# A Night in the Tavern

# Álvares de Azevedo

# A Night in the Tavern

Translated by Maurício Búrigo

With an introduction by Alcebiades Diniz Miguel

Universitas Press
Montreal

Universitas Press
Montreal

www.universitaspress.com

Modern Classics Editor: Cristina Artenie

First published in December 2025

Work published with the support of the National Library Foundation of
the Ministry of Culture of Brazil and the Guimarães Rosa Institute of the
Ministry of Foreign Affairs of Brazil.
*Obra publicada com o apoio da Fundação Biblioteca Nacional, do Ministério da Cultura
do Brasil, e do Instituto Guimarães Rosa, do Ministério das Relações Exteriores do
Brasil.*

Library and Archives Canada Cataloguing in
Publication

Title: A night in the tavern / Álvares de Azevedo ;
translated by Maurício Búrigo.
Other titles: Noite na taverna. English
Names: Azevedo, Manuel Antônio Alvares de,
1831-1852, author | Búrigo, Maurício, translator.
Description: Translation of: Noite na taverna.
Identifiers: Canadiana 2025025929X | ISBN
9781988963730 (softcover)
Subjects: LCGFT: Short stories.
Classification: LCC PQ9697.A965 N613 2025 |
DDC 869.3/3—dc23

# TABLE OF CONTENTS

# CHRONOLOGY

1831   *7 April. Abdication of Emperor Pedro I of the Empire of Brazil, succeeded by his son, the 5-year-old Pedro II.*
12 September. Manuel Antônio Álvares de Azevedo is born, the second son of Inácio Manuel Álvares de Azevedo and Maria Luísa Silveira da Mota Azevedo, in São Paulo, on the corner of Rua da Freira and Cruz Preta, today Senador Feijó and Quintino Bocaiúva.
*7 November. Lei Feijó, a law prohibiting slave trade in Brazil, never actually enforced until 1850. (See below.)*

1833   His family moves to Rio de Janeiro.

1835   One of his younger brothers dies.

1837   He is matriculated in a school in Niterói, State of Rio de Janeiro, where he is declared incapable of learning.

1840   He is matriculated in the Colégio Stoll, where he remains until 1844, and impresses the school principal with his intelligence.

1841   *18 July. Coronation of Pedro II as Emperor Pedro II of the Empire of Brazil.*

1844   After Professor Stoll abandons his school, Azevedo moves to São Paulo in the company of his uncle, José Inácio Silveira da Mota. There, in a course annexed to the Faculdade de Direito do Largo de São Francisco, he studies French, English and Latin. He does not complete the preparatory school to enter the juridical course for lack of minimum age.

1845   *29 January. "The Raven," by Edgar Allan Poe, is published in the* New York Evening Mirror.
Back to Rio de Janeiro, he is matriculated in the 5th year of the Colégio Pedro II, where he is a pupil of Barão de Planitiz (1814-1890), his professor of German; Gonçalves de Magalhães (1811-1882), Philosophy; Pereira da Silva, Greek; and Santiago Nunes Ribeiro (?-1847), Modern History, Rhetoric and Poetics.
*9 August. Aberdeen Act, or Slave Trade Act (United Kingdom), which gives the Royal Navy authority to stop and search suspicious Brazilian ships, and arrest slave traders, as part of the process of the suppression of slave trade in Africa and abolition of slavery in Brazil.*

1846   He receives a citation of honor at the conclusion of his school year.

1847   He receives his bachelor's degree in letters.

1848   10 March. He is matriculated in the Faculdade de Direito de São Paulo, where he makes friends with Bernardo Guimarães (1825-1884) and Aureliano Lessa (1828-1861), and is a colleague of José de Alencar (1829-1877). He shares lodgings with the first two and, inspired by Lord Byron, they found the Sociedade Epicuréia, which causes scandals at the time, for its supposed orgies and cult of Satan. He translates the fifth act of *Othello* by Shakespeare and *Parisina* by Byron. He composes "O conde Lopo" and various other poems. He also starts a correspondence with his friend Luís Antônio da Silva Nunes, from Rio Grande do Sul.

| 1849 | 11 August. As a second-year student, he delivers a speech at the academic session on the anniversary of the creation of juridical courses in Brazil, in which he discourses on the theme of "the civilizing mission of universities." |
|---|---|
| 1849 -1850 | During the 1849-1850 winter vacation, according to a letter (from 10 March 1850) to his friend Luís Nunes, he wrote "a novel of 200-odd pages; two poems, one with five and the other with two cantos; an analysis of Musset's *Rolla*; and some literary studies on the simultaneous march of civilization and poetry in Portugal, quite voluminous; a fragment of a poem in a very ancient language, more difficult to understand than [Gonçalves Dias's] *Sextilhas de Frei Antão*, in another taste, nevertheless, in the like manner of Chatterton's [fictional] Th. Rowley." |
| 1850 | In São Paulo, he actively participates in the literary life. 9 May. He delivers the inaugural speech for the Sociedade Acadêmica Ensaio Filosófico Paulistano, having founded its *Revista Mensal*. *4 September. Lei Eusébio de Queirós, a law prohibiting international slave trade, this time vigorously enforced in the country (See above.)* 12 September. Upon the suicide of a fifth-year colleague, Feliciano Coelho Duarte, he delivers a funeral speech. |
| 1851 | 15 November. With the death of another colleague, João Batista da Silva Pereira, he again delivers a funeral speech. Impressed with such an event, he writes to a sister about the presentiment that he wouldn't reach one more year of living. |

1852    25 April. Álvares de Azevedo dies in Rio de
        Janeiro. The cause of his death is controversial.
        On 10 March he had fallen off a horse and
        had been operated on for a tumor in the iliac
        fossa. This, as well as tuberculosis, have been
        rejected and today it is presumed that the cause
        of his death was diverticulitis. In his death
        certificate, the cause is recorded as "enteritis,
        with perforation of the intestine."

1853    Publication of *Obras de Manuel Antônio Álvares
        de Azevedo*, printed by the Tipografia Americana
        of José Justiniano da Rocha, and edited by
        Domingos Jaci Monteiro. The edition included
        both parts of "Lira dos vinte anos," nine
        poems gathered in "Poesias diversas," a preface
        by the editor, and a fragment of a letter of the
        poet to his friend Luís Nunes.

1855    Publication of the second volume of *Obras
        de Manuel Antônio Álvares de Azevedo*, printed
        by the Tipografia Universal of Laemmert e
        Cia., containing essays, speeches, eulogies of
        deceased colleagues, as well as "Macário" and
        "A Noite na Taverna."

1862    Edition in three volumes of *Obras de Manuel
        Antônio Álvares de Azevedo*, published by
        Garnier. New unpublished poems were added,
        besides "O poema do frade."

# Gifts of the Night
## Nocturnal Prose in *Night in the Tavern* by Álvares de Azevedo

### Alcebiades Diniz Miguel

*What hath night to do with sleep?*
(Milton 10)

*Night in the Tavern* was written under the pseudonym Job Stern—a curious combination of a biblical character's name and the German word for 'star'—and was only published posthumously in 1855. The author, Álvares de Azevedo, was a young poet who died prematurely: born in São Paulo in 1831, he passed away in Rio de Janeiro in 1852, before reaching the age of 21. Among his few completed works, the most famous is this collection of stories unified by a framed narrative structure like that of *One Thousand and One Nights*, *The Decameron*, or *The Canterbury Tales*, in which the short narrative's brief—and more intense—form facilitates narrative construction through the use of episodic effects within the narrative fabric itself. It is an old yet practical method of multiplying the different voices in the plot, allowing them to occupy both foreground and background in a narrative polyphony whose control becomes much more refined.

Álvares de Azevedo's *Night in the Tavern* is a collection of narratives interconnected by the context of their (re) production. Not only does Azevedo use the night as a backdrop, situating the moment when the narrators meet on a particular night; he goes further, as the night becomes a companion throughout this volume, enabling the characters and narrators of the interconnected plots to confess—or unleash their imaginations through—the darkest tales. The interconnected narratives are not merely imaginative exercises, which by their very nature are often nocturnal, but rather small tributes to the powers of the night. In this way, Álvares de Azevedo's brief and sophisticated narrative labyrinth, through peculiar paths, creates a unique vision of nocturnal life with enough force to supplant the diurnal one.

But what is the plot that drives the stories in *Night in the Tavern*? The five short narratives—preceded by a prologue and ending with an epilogue—that comprise the volume are evocative tales of horror and violence in the Romantic tradition, inheriting certain thematic elements established by the Gothic novel in the 18th century. The first narrative, titled "A Night of the Century," sets the backdrop and general framework of the plot: a tavern without a defined space or time, on an unspecified night, where, alongside the local regulars—prostitutes, drunks and libertines—, seven friends gather. These characters—Solfieri, Bertram, Gennaro, Claudius Hermann, Archibald, Arnold, and Johann—will narrate the five stories that form the core of *Noite na Taverna*. The names, which suggest diverse national origins, already express a kind of aesthetic declaration by Álvares de Azevedo—his critical stance toward the nativist and Indianist idyll that was prevalent in Brazilian Romanticism at the time. The long poem "I-Juca-Pirama" by Gonçalves Dias, published in 1851 (a year before Álvares de Azevedo's death), exemplified this tendency to idealize the Brazilian native as part of an exuberant, almost paradisiacal nature. Álvares de Azevedo—like Edgar Allan Poe in the United States—rejects this idyllic vision, seeking in his literary and poetic expression a reconnection with the literary tradition of his time, in addition to the Gothic novel, the sinister Romanticism *noir* exemplified by the narratives of Charles Nodier and E. T. A. Hoffmann. In fact, the latter is directly quoted at the end of the first chapter of *Night in the Tavern*, following several references in the preceding paragraphs to highly influential philosophers of the time, such as Schelling, Spinoza, Malebranche, and Hume.

By breaking with certain traditions already established in the Brazilian literature of his time, Azevedo adopted a different path—one glimpsed through philosophical and aesthetic influences such as German Idealism and Romanticism, the frenetic French narrative,[1] and the Gothic novel, which spread like wildfire throughout Europe from England. This three-landmark trajectory is evident in *Night in the Tavern*, both in its themes and in the development of its plots, characterized by excess and violence manifested through extreme actions, ranging from cannibalism to sexual violence. It is a dark, nocturnal path, disconnected from the issues mobilizing Brazilian society at the time. As mentioned above, this opposition aligns closely with the approach of Edgar Allan Poe in the United States and anticipates debates that would later unfold throughout Latin America, reaching a veritable peak in Argentina with the dispute between the *Martin Fierro* Group, led by Jorge Luis Borges, and the *Boedo* Group, with members like Roberto Arlt. These debates centered on subjectivity versus objectivity, stylized construction versus frank protest, and the necessity of a literature didactically aligned with contemporary discussions.

However, the connection between the author of *Night in the Tavern* and Edgar Allan Poe may be even more significant when considering how both understood their positions within their respective literary traditions. Poe is a singular figure in American

---

[1] Also the Spanish dark narrative tradition, as it would be possible to establish connections between *Night in the Tavern* and José Cadalso's posthumous *Noches lúgubres*, published by *Correo de Madrid* from 1789 to 1790. This work became influential as a precursor to the frenetic and brutal — sometimes derivative — school of dark Romanticism in Spain.

literature—an author both celebrated and, for a long time, regarded as an outsider. One hundred years ago, in his famous essay "Poe at Home and Abroad," Edmund Wilson highlighted the way in which Poe was perceived by critics throughout the nineteenth and twentieth centuries: "One of the most striking features of all this American criticism of Poe is its tendency to regard him as a freak" (Wilson 68). Interestingly, Poe himself never made great efforts to conform to the historical and social expectations placed upon him in American literature; the romantic realism he cultivated often led him to an abstract and universal interpretation of his work, one less tied to the moment or the needs of the *Zeitgeist*. Similarly, Álvares de Azevedo not only rejected the strong nativist tendencies of Brazilian literature in his time, but also questioned the necessity of a distinctly Brazilian literature with a specific identity, separate from the broader literary currents from Portugal, as noted by critic Antonio Candido: "Regarding this last aspect, let us remember that Álvares de Azevedo was a resolute anti-nationalist in terms of literature. According to him, our literature was part of Portuguese literature, and there was neither point nor advantage in proclaiming a distinct identity—an attitude that contrasted with the prevailing critical efforts of the time, constituting a paradox that must have been difficult and almost heroic to sustain" (Candido 13).

Indeed, it was a heroic effort—one that led to years of ostracism for Álvares de Azevedo. This eccentric stance toward Brazilian literature not only set him apart from the authors and critics of his generation, but also had lasting effects on how he was perceived within Brazilian literary history. Like Poe, he was considered a "freak," overlooked by subsequent historical developments and the avant-garde movements of the early 20th century.

Thus, the young Álvares de Azevedo's resolute stance became somewhat isolated within the landscape of Romantic Indianism. Unlike Poe, Borges and their contemporaries, the author's short life meant that the aesthetic influence of *Night in the Tavern* did not have immediate continuity. Consequently, *Night in the Tavern* remained an enigmatic work in Brazilian literature, encapsulated by the perspective expressed in the aforementioned essay, aptly titled "Education by the Night," by Antonio Candido: "we can only read his theater and his fiction in prose and verse as a collection of attempts and fragments" (22). These are therefore seen as the superficial whims of a rather immature young man; and whose squalid revolt was equally superficial and misguided. This reductive view was only challenged with the late revival of black romanticism in Brazil, first by marginal poets of the 1980s and later by an entire generation of local horror prose writers.

Thus, we can revisit some ideas outlined at the beginning of this brief introduction. Indeed, there is a pact with the night as an entity in *Night in the Tavern*, but in a different sense—one much closer to that envisioned by Novalis in the opening of his *Hymns to the Night*:

The giant world of the unresting constellations inhales it as the innermost soul of life, and floats dancing in its azure flood; the sparkling, ever-tranquil stone, the thoughtful, imbibing plant, and the wild, burning, multiform beast-world inhales it; but more than all, the lordly stranger with the meaning eyes, the swaying walk, and the sweetly closed, melodious lips. Like a king over earthly nature, it rouses every force to countless transformations, binds and unbinds innumerable alliances, hangs its heavenly form around every earthly substance. Its presence alone reveals the marvelous splendor of the kingdoms of the world. (Macdonald 3)

Contrary to Antonio Candido's interpretation, Azevedo's nocturnal prose does not merely adhere to a kind of "satanic pedagogy." For Romantics (and some marginalized groups alike), the night symbolizes the potential for consecration. In *A Night in the Tavern*, the vast expanse of black skies, which conceal heinous crimes, represents an unexplored territory—a utopia.

## WORKS CITED

Candido, Antonio. *A educação pela noite e outros ensaios.* São Paulo: Ática, 1989.

Macdonald, George. "From Novalis. *Hymns to the Night.*" *Rampolli: Growths from a Long-Planted Root.* London: Longmans, Green, 1897. 3-16.

Milton, John. *Comus.* Ed. William Bell. London and New York: Macmillan, 1891.

Wilson, Edmund. *A Literary Chronicle: 1920-1950.* New York: Doubleday, 1956.

# Translator's Note

Maurício Búrigo

Almost forty years ago, when I was first introduced to the poetry of Álvares de Azevedo via a brief textbook chapter on Brazilian Late Romanticism (so-called "ultra-Romanticism" at the time, though, in Azevedo's case, it should simply be called "Byronism") with its handful of poets, I could not have imagined that I would one day translate his *Noite na Taverna*. The things most people remember about Azevedo are his untimely death, the label with which the poets of that literary movement are associated, and those final lines of his ("Se eu morresse amanhã"), turned commonplace by textbooks and anthologies:

> If I were to die tomorrow, at least mine eyes
> Would be closed by my sister in sorrow;
> My mother of longing would die
> If I were to die tomorrow!
> (Azevedo, "Poesias Diversas")

*A Night in the Tavern* is a framed narrative, not unlike such famous models as *The Decameron* or *The Canterbury Tales*. The plots of the tales are often disconcerting. They are linked by a certain community of atmosphere, and furthermore by their oscillation between astonishment and catastrophe. Each new story seems to exceed the previous in terms of the extreme experiences related, which include incest, necrophilia, fratricide, cannibalism, betrayal, and murder—whose function in Romanticism was to show the virtual abysses and disharmonies of human nature as well as the frailty of conventions. Everything that happens in the tales is either obscured by the deepest night, assaulted by the inclemency of weather, hidden in dark recesses, lost on deserted labyrinthine streets or on winding paths through wooded mountains, all of which make up the arsenal of that "sublime beauty" reaching up to the transgressive and the "horrible." The tales are characterized by "the transgression of norms, the fascination for evil, and the play between desire and amorous possession . . . the presence of Satanism and Byronism is revealed as an inner force of the characters who populate the tales, a force which presents itself in rebelliousness, in irreverence, in vices, in eroticism, in irony . . . the characters are bandit-heroes, quite in Byronic molds . . . They are highly controversial young men: at the same time mocking and ironic, happy and sorrowful, vibrant and affectionate, sensuous and prudish, but above all, libertine and delinquent" (Cavalcante 4-5).

In the prologue for his dramatic piece *Macário*, Azevedo writes, as if in anticipation of the conception of the characters in *A Night in the Tavern* (provided the former was written before the latter) that: "It is difficult to mark the place where man stops and the animal begins, where the soul ceases and the instinct starts— where passion turns into ferocity. It is difficult to mark where the gallop of blood in the arteries, and the violence of pain in the skull, must stop. Nevertheless there must be and there is—a limit to the expansions of the actor so that there is neither exaggeration, nor degeneration of the role of a man into the role of a beast" (Azevedo, "Puff-Macário" 197). One of the foremost Brazilian scholars compared Azevedo's treatment of this stretching of the limits of human consciousness in drama and fiction: "*Noite na Taverna* is a research of these dubious frontiers, and its matter seems conceived and chosen by Satan as episode of a kind of *anti-Bildungsroman*, which he proposed for the formation (contrariwise) of his pupil . . . the possibility of purity and ideal being lost, there remains that ferocious path where man seeks to know the secret of his humanity by means of excess, to the extent of a behavior which denies all rules. This is not a matter of analysis anymore (like in *Macário*), but of facts, events and sentiments brought to the utmost of moral tension, up to the frontier of cruelty, perversion and crime, which test our diabolic possibilities" (Candido 15-16).

In his study of Alfred de Musset (see Azevedo, "Alfredo de Musset" 28), Álvares de Azevedo translates a fragment (the first eight lines) of the first stanza from Canto II of the poem *Rolla*, which, as an introduction to its hero, could very well sum up traits, temperaments, and dispositions of mind and spirit of some of the characters in *A Night in the Tavern*: "In Paris, of the world that most notorious town/ Of viciousness and sin, Jacques Rolla wore the crown./ A gambler in the lowest dens of crime and infamy,/ To noble impulses quite dead and lost was he./ Alone on Rolla's life dark passions held their sway,/ Nor did he strive to check those passions' willful play;/ Nay, more: as one who muses by a running stream,/ He smiling watched their course as in a changing dream" (Musset 6). In the same study on Musset, Azevedo translated the second and third stanzas from Canto I of *Childe Harold's Pilgrimage* by Byron. It is, however, his analysis of Byron's poems that might just as well have come out of the mouth of one of those gathered round a table at a tavern into the night, drinking and smoking while each told a most unlikely grotesque story, vociferated as a curse or, as it were, a fatality, in *A Night in the Tavern*: "Byron's poems are the mirror of that whole epoch. When an entire philosophy established the axiom of skepticism, and when the populace slept of God forgotten over the empty tombs of their kings—when the cross cracked on the frontispiece of cathedrals, and the livid and eburnean front of the crucifixes were splintered on the slabs of the profaned temple—one should not be surprised that poetry came to sing faith's funeral song over religion's corpse" (Azevedo, "Alfredo de Musset" 60-61).

WORKS CITED

Azevedo, Álvares de. "Alfredo de Musset, Jacques Rolla." *Obras de Manoel Antonio Alvares de Azevedo*. Vol. II. Rio de Janeiro: Typographia Universal Laemmert, 1855. 19-66.

Azevedo, Álvares de. "Poesias Diversas—Se eu morresse amanhã." *Obras de Manoel Antonio Alvares de Azevedo*. Vol. I. Rio de Janeiro: Typographia Americana, de J.J. da Rocha, 1853. 198.

Azevedo, Álvares de. "Puff – Macário." *Obras de Manoel Antonio Alvares de Azevedo*. Vol. II. Rio de Janeiro: Typographia Universal Laemmert, 1855. 195-283.

Candido, Antonio. "A educação pela noite." *A educação pela noite e outros ensaios*. São Paulo: Ática, 1989. 10-22.

Cavalcante, Maria Imaculada. "Álvares de Azevedo, um Contista Fantástico." *LINGUAGEM – Estudos e Pesquisas*, Catalão 10-11: 1 (2007), 1-23.

Musset, Alfred de. *Poems of Alfred de Musset*. Transl. by Marie Agathe Clarke. Vol. II. New York: Edwin C. Hill Co., 1905.

# A Night in the Tavern

How now, Horatio? You tremble, and look pale.
Is not this something more than phantasy?
What think you of it?
*HAMLET.* ACT I. SHAKESPEARE.[1]

[1] "How now, Horatio? you tremble, and look pale;/ Is not this something more than fantasy?/ What think you of it?" (*Hamlet* I, I, 52-54). The lines belong to Bernardo, one of the guards at Elsinore Castle.

# I

## A Night of the Century

Let's drink! not a song of longing!
Pains die in the drunkenness of life!
What matter dreams, illusions undone?
As flowers, they wither the same!
JOSÉ BONIFÁCIO.[2]

[2] José Bonifácio de Andrada e Silva, known as "the Younger" (1827-1886) was a friend of Azevedo, his fellow student at the School of Law. He had published a book of poetry in 1848 (*Rosas e Goivos*), but these lines must have been shared with Azevedo directly.

"Silence, lads! stop with these horrible ditties! Don't you see the women sleeping inebriated, emaciated like the dead? Don't you feel that the slumber of drunkenness weighs dark on those eyelids where beauty has sealed the look of voluptuousness?"

"Hush, Johann! while the women sleep and the fair-haired Arnold falters and falls asleep murmuring the orgy songs of Tieck,[3] what music is lovelier than the din of the saturnalia? When clouds run black in the sky like a flock of errant crows, and the moon fades like the light of a lamp over the whiteness of a beauty that sleeps, what better night than one spent in the reflection of goblets?"

"You're a fool, Bertram! it's not the moon that there goes emaciated: it's the lightning that passes and laughs, scornful of the agonies of the people that die, of the sobs that follow the processions of cholera!"

"Cholera! and what does it matter? Is there not life enough for now in the veins of

[3] Ludwig Tieck (1773-1853) is one of the founders of German Romanticism, best remembered today for his fiction and his translations from Shakespeare. The "fair-haired Arnold" is a clear reference to Tieck's Gothic fairy tale "Der blonde Eckbert" (1797), best known in English as "The Fair-Haired Eckbert" (a title given by Thomas Carlyle to his 1827 translation).

man? does fever not still bubble in the waves of wine? does the lamp of life not sparkle with all its fire in the lantern of the skull?"

"Wine! wine! Don't you see that the goblets are empty and we drink the vacuum, like a somnambulist?"

"It's the Fichteanism of inebriation![4] spiritualist, drink to the immateriality of inebriation!"

"Oh! empty! my glass is empty! Hey, tavernkeeper! Don't you see that the bottles are dry? Don't you know, you wretch, that the lips of the bottle are like those of a woman: they are only worthy of kisses while the fire of wine or the fire of love sprinkles them with lava?"

"The wine is gone from the glasses, Bertram, but the smoke still undulates in the pipes! After the vapors of wine, the vapors of smoke! Gentlemen, on behalf of all our reminiscences, of all our dreams that will lie, of all our hopes that will fade, one last toast! The tavernkeeper there brought us more

[4] Immaterialism was a term first associated with George Berkeley (1685-1753), but then also (rather incorrectly) applied to subjective idealists like Kant (1724-1804) and the post-Kantian Johann Gottlieb Fichte (1762-1814), although Fichte did not deny the existence of matter (and hence of things-in-themselves, independent of human observation) outside of consciousness (like Berkeley) or the possibility of knowing a thing-in-itself beyond its appearances (like Kant), but only suggested that we cannot rationalize on the thing-in-itself.

wine: a toast! Smoke is the image of idealism, it mirrors all that is most vaporous in that spiritualism which speaks of the immortality of the soul! and so, to the smoke of the Antilles,[5] to the immortality of the soul!"

"Bravo! bravo!"

A triple *hurrah!* responded to the half-inebriated lad.

One of the drinking buddies rose amidst the uproar: contrasted with his youthful face were the wrinkles on his brow and the purpleness of his convulsive lips. The lights of the feast threw silver glints through his hair. He spoke:

"Hush, you damned! the immortality of the soul! you pathetic fools! seeing that the soul is beautiful, why can't you conceive that this ideal might also become sludge and putrefaction just like the lovely face of the dead virgin; can't you believe it dies? Fools! have you perchance never spent a night of vigil by the bedside of a corpse? And then have you not doubted that he was dead, and that that chest and that brow would pulsate again, that those eyelids would open, that it was only the opium of sleep which had rendered that man mute? Immortality of the

[5] Tobacco smoking was first reported by Columbus's men on Monday, 5 November 1492, on the island of Cuba, the largest of the Greater Antilles.

soul! and why not dream of that of flowers, of the breeze, and of perfumes as well? Oh! a thousand times no! the soul is not like the moon—forever young, naked and lovely in her eternal virginity!—life is nothing but the haphazard gathering of molecules drawn to each other: what used to be the body of woman might turn into a cypress or into a cloud of miasmas; what used to be the body of worm will be whitened into the calyx of the flower or onto the brow of the fairest and loveliest child. As Schiller has said, the atom of Plato's intelligence has gone, perhaps, into the heart of an impure being.[6] Therefore I'll tell you: if you understand immortality as metempsychosis, well! I may believe it a little; but as Platonism, no!"

"Solfieri! you're daft! materialism is as arid as a desert, 'tis as benighted as a tomb! Such cold beliefs have you in store for our

[6] In Friedrich Schiller's essay (organized in the form of a short philosophical dialogue) "The Walk under the Linden Trees" (first published in the *Wirtembergisches Repertorium der Litteratur*, which Schiller co-edited, in 1782), the pessimistic Wollmar suggests that "The atom which in Plato's brain seemed vivified by the thought of Deity, which vibrated with mercy in Titus' heart, is now perhaps quivering with beastly lust in the breast of some modern Sardanapalus, or is scattered about by buzzards as the carrion of some hung scoundrel!" (in the 1861 translation by Charles J. Hempel). Titus was a Roman emperor praised for the help he offered the survivors of an eruption of the Vesuvius; Sardanapalus, king of Assyria, was famed for his decadence.

brows scorched by the sultry sun of life, for our pates turned hoary by old age? Give us the dreams of spiritualism!"

"Archibald! right you are, all this is but a dream! In another time my foremost dream was the pure spirit[7] kneeling in its silvery mantle, in an ocean of aromas and lights! Illusions! reality is the fever of the libertine, goblet in hand, lasciviousness on his lips, and the half-naked woman, trembling and tingling on his knees."

"Blasphemy! and don't you believe in anything else? has your skepticism knocked down all the statues of the temple, even that of God?"

"God! believe in God! aye, when the inner cry reveals him in the cold hours of fear—in the hours one shivers with fright and death, humid death, seems to rub against us! On the raft of the shipwrecked, on the scaffold, in the desert—always bathed in the cold sweat of terror, that's where the belief in God comes from!—To believe in him as the utopia of the absolute good, the sun of light and love, very well! But if you understand him as the idols

[7] "Pure spirit" was a concept variously understood by several German Idealists. The reference here is probably to Fichte who, in his *System of Ethics* spoke of "my drive as a natural being and my tendency as a pure spirit," although (unlike the speaker here) he saw them as "one and the same original drive, which constitutes my being, simply viewed from two different sides."

which men have raised bathed in blood, and which fanaticism kisses in their inanimateness of five-thousand-year-old marble—I do not believe in him!"

"What about the holy books?"

"Misery! when you come to me to speak of poetry, I will tell you: there are pages there inspired by the ardent nature of that land, such as not even Homer had dreamed of—such as the entire humanity, kneeling on the tombs of the past, will never again remember! But when you speak to me of religious truths, of holy visions, of the ravings of that stupid people, I'll tell you—misery! misery! three times misery! All that is false: they lie like the mirages of the desert!"

"You're drunk, Johann! Atheism is insanity, like Schelling's mystical idealism,[8] like the pantheism of Spinoza the Jew,[9] like the faithful Esotericism of Malebranche in

[8] "Mystical idealism" was actually applied by Kant to Berkeley's philosophy (see note 4). Friedrich Wilhelm Joseph Schelling (1775-1854) was a German philosopher who actually espoused views often seen as pantheistic in his last major work (which bears the influence of such German mystics as Jakob Boehme and F.X. von Baader), *Philosophical Inquiries into the Essence of Human Freedom* (1809), in which he equated God with Nature and saw the former as self-evolving.

[9] Baruch Spinoza (1632-1677) was a Dutch philosopher who wrote in Latin. His pantheism was best expressed in his *Ethics* (1677), where he argued that God is Nature and Nature is God.

his dreams of the vision in God.[10] The true philosophy is Epicureanism.[11] Hume said it well: for man, the end is pleasure.[12] Hence you see that it's the sensitive element which dominates.[13] And so let's rise, we who have grown yellow in the faded nights of insane study, and have seen that science is false and elusive, that it lies and intoxicates like a woman's kiss."

"Well! very well! that's a respectable *toast!*"[14]

"I want all of you to stand up, and with your heads uncovered say: To Pan God of

[10] Nicolas Malebranche (1638-1715), a French theologian whose main philosophical idea is that of the "vision in God," according to which human beings can know objects through their archetypes (similar to Plato's "ideas"), but since these are actually of divine origin, they can only be "seen" in God through revelation.

[11] Epicurus (341-270 BC) defined the absence of pain and fear as the greatest pleasure and the latter as the ultimate goal in life. Epicurean ideas were revived in the 17th and 18th centuries.

[12] David Hume (1711-1776) was a Scottish philosopher. The dichotomy pleasure/pain (though he preferred good/evil) plays a central part in his writings, especially in *A Treatise of Human Nature* (1739-1740).

[13] A conflation of modern epicureanism and the importance attached by someone like Hume to pleasure (see notes 11-12) and Hume's own empiricism, i.e., the idea that both our knowledge and our morals are based on sensory experience as well as experimental procedures.

[14] The English word "toast" is used here (in italics) in the Portuguese original.

nature, the one whom antiquity called Bacchus, son of a god's thighs and a woman's love,[15] and whom we call better by his name—wine."

"To wine! to wine!"

The glasses fell empty onto the table.

"Now hear me, gentlemen! between a toast and a puff of smoke, when heads burn and elbows stretch out on the tablecloth wet with wine, like the arms of a butcher on the dripping chopping block, what suits us is a gory tale, one of those fantastic stories—like Hoffmann spouted in the golden glare of Johannisberg!"[16]

"A dreadful story, isn't it, Archibald?" spoke a pasty lad who on hearing that call had lifted his yellowish head.

"Well then, I'll tell you a story. But, as for this one, you may shiver as you like, you

[15] Dionysus (called Bacchus by the Romans) was a major deity in Greek mythology. Son of Zeus and Persephone (or Demeter), he was reborn as the son of a human mother (Semele). He was credited as the inventor of wine during his second incarnation. Pan was a lesser (though older) deity (a spirit of nature), but he was later identified with Dionysus in the later Dionysian Mysteries, especially in the Roman version known as Bacchanalia.

[16] Johannisberg is a village and a vineyard in Germany, famous for its Riesling wine. E.T.A. Hoffmann (1776-1822) was a German Romantic novelist and short-story writer, famous for his Gothic and satiric fictions. He was an avid consumer of good wines and recommended Johannisberg in his stories.

may sweat cold thick beads of terror on your forehead. It's not a tale, it's a remembrance from the past."

"Solfieri! Solfieri! here you come with your fantasies!"

"Tell it!"

Solfieri spoke: the rest remained silent.

# II

## Solfieri

... Yet one kiss on yon pale clay,
And those lips once so warm—my heart! my heart!
BYRON, CAIN.[17]

[17] From Byron' 1821 play *Cain* (Act III, scene i). These are the last lines spoken by Zillah (Abel's wife), as she is persuaded by Adam to leave her husband's body behind. The epigraph is in English in the original, but the punctuation and one word ("yon," which appears as "your" in all Portuguese editions) have been corrected here.

"You know it. Rome is the city of fanaticism and perdition: in the alcove of the priest sleeps at ease the concubine; above the bed of the harlot hangs the livid Crucifix. It's a distillation of blasphemous joy which mingles sacrilege with the convulsion of love, the lascivious kiss with the intemperance of faith.

"It was in Rome. One night the moon went by as beautiful as it always does in summer, across that lukewarm sky; the freshness of the waters exhaled like a sigh from the bed of the Tiber. The night went by, beautiful.—I was strolling by myself across the ____ bridge. The lights went off one by one in the palazzi, the streets became deserted, and the sleepy moon hid itself in a bed of clouds. A woman's shadow appeared in a solitary, dark window. It was a white shape.— That woman's face was like that of a pale statue under the moon. Down her face, like drips from a dropped goblet, rolled threads of tears.

"I leaned against the corner of a palazzo.—The vision disappeared in the darkness of the window, and from there a song poured out. It was not just a melodious voice: there was in that singing as if a weeping of frenzy, as if a moaning of insanity: that voice was somber like that of the wind in the cemeteries at night, singing lullabies to the withered flowers of death.

"Then the song hushed. The woman appeared at the door. She seemed to check whether there was anyone on the streets. She saw nobody—she left. I followed her.

"It was getting later and later into the night: the moon had vanished into the sky, and the rain fell with heavy drops: only I felt falling on my face thick tears of water, like the weeping of orphans over a grave.

"We walked for a long time through the labyrinth of the streets: at last, she stopped: we were in a field.

"Here—there—everywhere there were crosses rising amidst the grass. She knelt down. She seemed to be sobbing: around her passed the night birds.

"I don't know if I fell asleep: I only know that when dawn broke I found myself alone in the cemetery. Nevertheless, the pale creature was not an illusion—the heather and the hemlocks of the graveyard were flattened next to a cross.

"The cold of the night, that slumber spent in the rain, caused me a fever. In my delirium, that whiteness of a woman came by and by, those sobs came moaning too, and all that reverie was lost in the softest of songs…

"A year later I returned to Rome. In the kisses of women nothing satisfied me: in the sleep of satiety that vision came to me...

"One night, and after an orgy, I left Countess Barbora sleeping in her bed. I gave a last look at that naked and dormant figure with fever on the face and lasciviousness on the wet lips, still moaning in her dreams as in the voluptuous agony of love.—I went out.—I don't know if the night was clear or black—I just know that my head was scalding with ebriety. The glasses had remained empty on the table: from the lips of that creature I had drunk the wine of delight to the last drop...

"When I came to, I was in a dark place: the stars cast their white rays through the windowpanes of a temple. The lights of four slender candles stroke upon a half-opened coffin. I opened it: it was a maiden's. That white of the shroud, the garlands of death on her forehead, on that livid and dim complexion, the glassiness of those imperfectly closed eyes... she was dead; and all those features reminded me of a lost fancy...—Was she the angel of the cemetery?—I shut the doors of the church, which, for some unknown reason, I had found open. I took the corpse in my arms out of the coffin. It was as heavy as lead...

21

"Do you know the story of the beheaded Mary Stuart and of the executioner, 'the headless corpse and the heartless man,' as told by Brantôme?[18]—It was a peculiar idea the one I had. I took her on my lap. I planted a thousand kisses on her lips. She was that beautiful: I tore off her shroud, stripped her of veil and chaplet, as the bridegroom strips them from the bride. It was the purest form. My dreams had never conjured up such a perfect statue. It was indeed a statue: so white was she. The light of the candlesticks gave her that amber pallor which glazes ancient marble. My joy was ardent—I sat that vigil in perdition. The dawn was now passing limply through the windows. To that heat in my bosom, to the fever on my lips, to the convulsion of my love, the pale maiden seemed to revive. Suddenly she opened her sluggish eyes.—A shadowy light illumined them like a star through the mist—she held me tight into her arms—a sigh waving across her bluish lips… At once it was not death—it was a swoon. And yet, in the tightness of that

[18] Brantôme (c.1540-1614) was a French courtier and author. He knew Mary Stuart (1542-1587), though he did not witness her execution, which he recounts in his *Vies des Dames Illustres*. The quotation, however, comes from the last page of Alexandre Dumas's *Les Stuarts* (1840), in which Brantôme's account is delicately summarized: "Brantôme relates that a vile thing happened then between this heartless man and this headless corpse."

embrace there was something horrific. The tombstone bed where I had spent an hour of drunkenness chilled me. With great pains was I able to detach myself from that tight hold of her bosom... In that instant she awakened...

"Haven't you ever heard of catalepsy? It's a horrible nightmare, which haunts one who awakens walled up in a sepulcher; a frozen dream in which one feels one's limbs paralyzed, and the face bathed in alien tears, unable to reveal life!

"The maiden revived little by little. She had fainted as she woke. I cloaked myself with my cape and took her in my arms, wrapped in her shroud like a child. As I approached the door, I bumped into a body: I stooped; I looked: it was some gravedigger from the churchyard who had fallen asleep there drunk, forgetting to lock the door...

"I left.—As I crossed the square, I encountered a patrol.

"'What are you carrying there?'

"It was quite late at night—perhaps they thought I was a thief.

"'It's my wife who has fainted...'

"'A woman!... What about these long white clothes? Are you perhaps a body snatcher?'

"One guard approached. He touched her forehead—it was cold.

"'This is a dead woman…'

"I brought my lips to hers. I felt a lukewarm breath.—It was life, still.

"'Look,' I said.

"The guard brought his lips to hers: his coarse lips grazed the maiden's. If I sensed the popping sound of a kiss… the dagger was already bare in my cold hands…

"'Good night, lad: you can go on,' he said.

"I walked away.—I was tired. I was struggling to carry my burden—and I felt the maiden was going to wake up. Fearful that they would hear her scream and come to my aid, I hurried with even greater exertion…

"When I went through the door, she woke. The first sound that came out of her mouth was a scream of fear…

"As soon as I closed the door, someone knocked. It was a band of libertines, companions of mine, who had returned from the orgy.—They demanded I open the door.

"I locked the maiden in my bedroom, and I opened the door.

"Half an hour later I left them in the living room, still drinking. The haze of drunkenness prevented them from noticing my absence.

"When I entered the room where the maiden was I saw her standing. She was laughing with a convulsive laughter like that of madness, and as cold as the blade of a sword. It pierced me with pain to hear her.

"Two days and two nights she spent with such a fever... There was no healing that delirium, nor that laughter of frenzy.—She died after two nights and two days of delirium.

"At night I left; I went to meet a sculptor who worked perfectly with wax, and I paid him for a statue of the maiden.

"When the sculptor left, I lifted the marble bricks from my bedroom, and with my hands I dug a tomb there.—I took her for the last time into my arms, pressed her to my bosom, silent and cold, kissed her and covered her, asleep in eternal slumber, with the linen from her bed.—I closed her in her tomb and spread my bed over it.

"For one year—night after night—I slept over the slabs that covered her... One day the sculptor brought me his work.—I paid for it and paid for the secret...

"Don't you remember, Bertram, the white shape of a woman that you glimpsed through the veil of my curtains? Don't you remember I answered that it was a virgin who slept?"

"And who was that woman, Solfieri?"

"Who was she? her name?"

"Who cares about a word when they feel the wine burning their lips? who asks the name of the prostitute one has slept with, and felt her dying with one's kisses, when there's no need to write it onto the gravestone?"

Solfieri filled a goblet.—He drank it. He was about to rise from the table when one of the guests took him by the arm.

"Solfieri, isn't this all just a tale?"

"By hell, no! by my father who was a count and a bandit, by my mother who was a beautiful Messalina[19] of the streets—by damnation, no! Since I myself pressed down that woman into her earthen grave—I swear to you—I have kept her chaplet as an amulet. Here it is!"

He opened his shirt, and they saw round his neck a garland of withered flowers.

"You see it? as withered and dry as that skull of hers!"

[19] Messalina (c.17/20-48) was a Roman empress, wife of Claudius. Due to her reputation for promiscuity, her name has become a byword for a prostitute or a slut.

# III

## Bertram

But why should I for others groan,
When none will sigh for me?
CHILDE HAROLD I.[20]

[20] English in the original. From Byron's *Childe Harold's Pilgrimage* (I, xiii, 184-185), first published in 1812. The lines are from the hero's "last 'Good Night,'" a poem-within-the-poem in which Harold (in dialogue with his young page) says goodbye to his native land. The comma at the end of the first line, which was missing in the Portuguese original, has been inserted here. In the first Brazilian editions, "groan" was also misspelled as "groon."

Another guest stood up.

It was a redhead with a white complexion, one of those phlegmatic creatures who will not hesitate, when they stumble upon a corpse, to grasp at it.

He emptied the glass full of wine, and with his beard in his white hands, his sea-green eyes glaring steadily, he spoke:

"You know, a woman drove me to perdition. She was the one who brought me into the fever of orgies and faded my lips with the ardor of wines and the softness of her kisses: who made me this pale through long dissolute nights of insomnia at the gaming tables, and in the folly of the convulsive embraces with which she held me to her bosom! She is the one, you know, who made me fight three duels in one day with my three best friends, open three tombs for those who loved me most in life—and then, then feel lonely and abandoned in the world, like the infanticide who killed her son, or that miserable Moor next to his pallid Desdemona![21]

"Well then, I'll tell you a story which begins with a recollection of that woman...

[21] Desdemona's "whiter skin . . . than snow" is mentioned in Othello's famous monologue at the beginning of Act V, Scene ii.

"There was in Cadiz[22] a damsel—lovely with that dark complexion of the Andalusians which you couldn't see—beneath the fringes of her satin mantilla, with delicate soles, hands of alabaster, eyes that shine, and lips like Alexandria roses[23]—without dreaming delirious dreams of them during long ardent nights!

"Andalusian women! you're so beautiful! if the wine, the nights of your land, the moonlight of your nights, your flowers, and your perfumes are sweet, and pure, and intoxicating—you are even more so! Oh! for this ceaselessly infectious joy of a fiery existence, I could never forget you!

"Gentlemen! there we have wine from Spain, fill the glasses—to Spanish ladies!

. . . . . . . . . . . . . . . . . . . . . . . . . . . . . . . . . .
. . . . . . . . . . . . . . . . . . . . . . . . . . . . . . . . . .

"I loved this young woman very much, by the name of Angela. When I was determined to marry her, when after long nights wasted in the sultry shade waiting for a wave, a farewell, a flower—when after so much desire and so

---

[22] Cadiz is one of the major cities in Andalusia, one of the fifteen historic regions created in 1833. It is a port on the Atlantic Ocean, as it lies west of the Strait of Gibraltar.

[23] Most commonly known as Damask or Damascene roses (also: Old Castilian roses).

much hope I drew her first kiss—I had to depart from Spain to Denmark, where my father was calling me.

"It was a night of sobs and tears, of weeping and hoping, of kisses and promises, of love, of voluptuousness in the present and of dreams of the future... I departed. It was two years later that I returned. As I entered my father's house, he was dying: he knelt on his bed and thanked God he could still see me: he placed his hands on my head, bathed my forehead with tears—they were his last—then he collapsed, put his hands on his chest, and with his eyes on me, he murmured—'God!'

"His voice was choking in his throat: everybody was crying.

"I was also crying—but it was from missing Angela...

"As soon as I could liquidate my fortune, I put the money in the Bank of Hamburg[24] and left for Spain.

"When I returned, Angela was married, and had a son...

"However, my love was not dead! Neither was hers!

"Quite ardent still were those hours of love and tears, of longings and kisses, of dreams and maledictions, for us to forget one another.

---

[24] The Hamburger Bank, which existed from 1619 to 1875.

. . . . . . . . . . . . . . . . . . . . . . . . . . . . . . . . . . . .
. . . . . . . . . . . . . . . . . . . . . . . . . . . . . . . . . . .

"One night, two figures emerged in the shadows of a garden, the leaves shivered with the ruffling of a dress, the breezes sobbed with the sobs of two lovers, and the perfume of violets which they treaded on, of roses and honeysuckles which they cleared around them, was even sweeter, lost in the perfume of the loose hair of a woman...

"That night—it was madness! it was a few hours of fiery dreams! and how quickly they passed! After that night another followed, and another... and many nights the leaves rustled with the grazing of a mysterious footstep, and the wind became intoxicated with delight on our pallid brows...

"But one day her husband found out all about it: he wanted to play Othello with her. The lunatic!...

"It was late at night: I was expecting to see the shadow of an angel pass by the white curtains. As I walked past, a voice called me. I entered—Angela, with bare feet, loose dress, disheveled hair and burning eyes, took me by the hand... I felt her hand wet... Dark was the stair we climbed: I rubbed my hand, moistened by hers, over my lips.—It had the taste of blood.

"'Blood, Angela! Whose blood is this?'

"The Spanish woman tossed her long black hair and laughed.

"We entered a room. She went out to fetch some light and left me in the dark.

"I groped for a place to sit: I touched a table. But as I passed my hand over it I felt it bathed in moisture: further, I felt a head as cold as snow and wet with a thick and somewhat coagulated liquid. It was blood...

"When Angela came back with the light, I saw... it was horrible. Her husband was decapitated.

"It was a gypsum statue washed in blood... On the chest of the murdered man lay a child, face down. She raised him by the hair... He was dead, too: the blood that ran off the ripped veins of his chest mixed with that of his father!

"'You see, Bertram, this was my gift: now it will be, dark as it may, a dream from my past. I am yours, and yours alone. It was for you that I had the strength to commit such crime... Come, all is ready, let us flee. The future is ours!'

. . . . . . . . . . . . . . . . . . . . . . . . . . . . . . . . . . . . .
. . . . . . . . . . . . . . . . . . . . . . . . . . . . . . . . . . .

"It was insane, my life with that woman! It was endless travelling. Angela dressed like a man: she made a handsome youth like that. Besides, she was like all the libertine lads who at the tables of orgy stroke their goblet against hers.—She already drank like an Englishwoman, smoked like a sultana, mounted a horse like an Arab, and shot firearms like a Spaniard.

"When the vapor of liquors burned my brow, she would hold me on her knees, take a mandolin and sing me the songs of her land...

"Our days were cast to sleep like pearls to love: our nights, indeed, were lovely!

. . . . . . . . . . . . . . . . . . . . . . . . . . . . . . . . . . . . .
. . . . . . . . . . . . . . . . . . . . . . . . . . . . . . . . . . .

"One day she departed: she departed, but left my lips yet burned by hers, and my heart filled with the germ of vices she had cast there. She departed; but her memory remained like the ghost of an evil angel close to my bed.

"I wanted to forget her with gambling, drinking, and the passion for duels. I became a cheater at cards, lost to women and orgies, a terrible and heartless swordsman.

. . . . . . . . . . . . . . . . . . . . . . . . . . . . . . . . . . . . .
. . . . . . . . . . . . . . . . . . . . . . . . . . . . . . . . . . .

"One night I had fallen inebriated by the doors of a palace: the horses of a carriage trampled over me as they passed and smashed my head against the pavement. Succor came from the palace. Then I was loved: the family consisted of an old noble widower and an eighteen-year-old rare beauty. It was not love, for sure, what I felt for her—I don't know what it was—it was an infernal fatality. The poor innocent loved me; and I, received as God's guest under the old hidalgo's roof, dishonored his daughter, stole her, fled with her... And the old man had to mourn his gray hair tainted by the daughter's dishonor, unable to take revenge.

"Then I grew tired of that woman.— Satiety is terribly dull.—One night when I was gambling with Siegfried the pirate, after losing her last jewels, I sold her.

"The girl poisoned Siegfried the very first night, and drowned herself...

. . . . . . . . . . . . . . . . . . . . . . . . . . . . . . . . . . . .
. . . . . . . . . . . . . . . . . . . . . . . . . . . . . . . . . . .

"There it is, who I am: if I wanted to tell you long stories of my life, your vigils would be much too brief...

"One day—it was in Italy—sated with wine and women, I was going to commit suicide. The night was dark and I went alone to the beach. I climbed a rock: thence, my last utterance was a blasphemy, my last farewell a curse... *my last*, I misspeak; because I felt myself lifted from the waters by my hair.

"Then, in the vertigo of hypoxia, the craving for life awakened within me. At first it had been a blindness, a cloud before my eyes, like those of someone who toils in the dark. The thirst for life became ardent: I clutched the one who was helping me: so much so, in one word, that I unwittingly killed him. Weary with the effort, I fainted...

"When I recovered my senses I was on a ship's launch with sailors rowing out to sea. Then I knew that my savior had died suffocated because of me. It was fate, a dark one; and so I laughed: I laughed while the sons of the sea were weeping.

"We reached a corvette[25] that was weighing anchor.

"The captain was a handsome man. Down his red cheeks hung the curly blond hair, where old age had bleached some of its locks.

"He asked me:

"'Who are you?'

"'A wretch who can't live on earth, and whom they didn't let die in the sea.'

"'So, would you like to come aboard?'

"'Unless you'd rather throw me into the sea.'

"'I wouldn't do that: you have a fine figure. I'll take you with me.—You'll serve...'

[25] A small warship with a single deck of guns.

"'Serve!'—and I laughed: then I answered him, coldly: 'Let me throw myself into the sea…'

"'You don't want to serve? Do you want to travel with your arms crossed, then?'

"'No: when the time comes for maneuvers, I'll sleep; but when time comes for combat, no one will be braver than me…'

"'Very well: I like you,' said the old sea dog. 'Now that we are acquainted, tell me your name and your story.'

"'My name is Bertram. My story? Listen: the past is a grave: ask the tomb the story of the corpse! it will keep its secret… it will only tell you that in its bosom lies a rotting body! You will read a name on the gravestone—and no more!'

"The captain knit his brow, then went ahead to lead the ship's maneuver.

"The captain had brought on board a lovely young woman. A pale creature, she would have appeared to a poet as the angel of hope sleeping forgotten amid the waves. The sailors respected her: when on moonlit nights she rested her arm on the railing and her cheek on her hand, those who passed by her uncovered their heads, respectful. Nobody had ever seen her throw looks of pride or heard her speak words of anger: she was a saint.

"She was the captain's wife.

"Between that brutal and valiant man, a fierce king of the high seas, wedded, like the Doges of Venice to the Adriatic,[26] to his elegant corvette—between that man and that Madonna there was the love of men whose beating hearts, on long nights, open up to the moons of the solitary ocean, who sleep thinking of her in the cold of the waves and the heat of the tropics, who sigh in the watch hours, late at night, on the railing of the ship, remembering her in the mists of darkness, in the clouds of the afternoon... Poor fools! it seems those men love a lot! On board I heard from many sailors about their simple loves: they were blonde maidens from Brittany and Normandy, or some Spanish girl with black hair, glanced at as she passed—seated on the beach with her basket of flowers—or asleep amid scented orange groves—or dancing the lascivious fandango[27] at outdoor parties, in the dew of night! There were many faces around me, rugged and tanned by the sea sun, that were bathed in tears...

[26] The city of Venice (or rather its leader and representative, the doge of Venice) was ritually married to the Adriatic Sea every year until 1797. The ceremony is reenacted today by the mayor of Venice.

[27] The supposed lasciviousness of the Spanish fandango was well documented in the 18th century by travelers through the Iberian peninsula (who also noted influences from the West Indies), though its exact movements are not well known.

"Let's get back to the story:—The captain worshipped her like a madman—a little less than his honor, a little more than his corvette.

"And she—she, amid her melancholy, her sadness and her pallor—she smiled sometimes when she mused alone—but it was so sad a smile that it hurt. Poor thing!

"A poet would have loved her down on his knees. One night—I was certainly drunk—I made her some verses. In the languid poem I had poured a precious and limpid essence which had not yet been polluted in the world...

"In good faith, I cried when I made those verses. One day, months later, I read them, laughed at them and at myself and threw them into the sea... It was the last leaf of my candor which I was casting into oblivion...

"Now, fill up your glasses—what I'm about to tell you is dark: it's a horrible memory, like nightmares in the ocean.

"With her tears, with her smiles, with her moist eyes, and her breasts swollen with sighs—that woman drove me mad at night. It was like a new life born full of desires, when I believed they were all dead like children drowned in blood at birth.

"I loved her: why tell you more? She loved me as well. Once, the moon moved clear and serene over the waters—the clouds were white like a veil embroidered with pearls of the night—the wind sang through the ropes.

I drank, in the purity of that moonlight, in the cool of that night, a thousand kisses from her face wet with tears, as one drinks the dew from a brimming lily. That palpitating bosom, its satiny contour, I pressed them to me...

"The captain was sleeping.

. . . . . . . . . . . . . . . . . . . . . . . . . . . . . . . . . . . . .
. . . . . . . . . . . . . . . . . . . . . . . . . . . . . . . . . . .

"Once at dawn the lookout signaled a vessel. Half an hour later he suspected it was a pirate ship...

"We came closer and closer. The shot of a blank charge by the corvette demanded the flag. They didn't respond. A second shot was fired—nothing. Then the shot of a cannonball reached the waters next to the unknown ship like a gauntlet in a duel. The ship that until then had kept an opposite bearing to ours, now steered its prow against ours, then turned and showed us its smoky flank: a flash of lightning ran through the pirate's batteries—a blast followed it—and a cloud of pellets came to die near the corvette.

"She wasn't motionless, but turned on her broadside: the ships now stood side by side.—At the discharge of the man-o'-war the pirate ship shuddered as if it was about to sink.

. . . . . . . . . . . . . . . . . . . . . . . . . . . . . . . . . . . .
. . . . . . . . . . . . . . . . . . . . . . . . . . . . . . . . . . .

"The pirate ship fled: the corvette gave chase: volleys were then exchanged, stronger, from both sides.

"At last, the pirate ship seemed to give in. The two ships came alongside each other as if ready for broadside combat. The corvette vomited its crew aboard the enemy ship. The battle turned bloody—it was a slaughterhouse; the deck of the ship was slippery with so much blood: the sea was agonizing, full of foam, with so many corpses floating. In a moment, smoke was seen coming from the hold. The pirate ship had set the gunpowder on fire… Only by an intrepid maneuver could the corvette distance itself from danger. But the explosion did it great damage. A few minutes later the pirate's ship blew up in the air. It was a dreadful scene to see the men hurled into the air and falling down into the ocean, amid that blazing fire, the roar of the gunpowder, and the flames glaringly reverberating upon the waters.

"Some, half-burned, threw themselves into the water, others, with grazed limbs and the skin flayed from their bodies, still swam in horrible pain and died writhing in curses.

"One league away from the combat scene there was a wild beach, jagged with steep rocks... There the pirates who were able to escape saved themselves.

"And during that time, while the captain fought like a brave man, I dishonored him like a coward.

"I don't know what befell in all the time that elapsed. It was a vision of damned joys—it was the loves of Satan and Eloa,[28] of death and of life—on a seabed.

"When I awakened one day from that dream, the ship was stranded on a sandbar: the creaking of the keel biting the sand froze us all—my awakening was to a cry of agony...

"Hey, woman! damned tavernkeeper, don't you see that the wine is gone?

"Then there was a horrible scene! We were on a raft in the middle of the sea. You who have read *Don Juan*,[29] who have perhaps made of that poison your Bible, who have slept the nights of satiety, like me, with the face upon it—and have so many times seen the dawn with the eyes still fixed on it—you know how much strained by horror are those

[28] Allusion to the epic poem *Eloa, or the Sister of the Angels* (1824) by French Romantic author Alfred de Vigny (1797-1863). Eloa is an angel who falls in love with a stranger who turns out to be Lucifer.

[29] Part of Canto the Second of Byron's *Don Juan* (stanzas xxvii-c) narrates the misadventures of shipwrecked sailors.

men thrown into the sea, in a horizonless sea, in the sway of the waters, which seem to suffocate their scorn with the cold muteness of fatality!

"One night, the storm came—there was just enough time to secure our ammunition... One must see the Ocean roaring in the dark like a pride of hungry lions to really know what a squall is—one must see it from a raft in the light of the storm, with the blasphemies of those who don't believe and curse, with the tears of those who hope and despair, with the sobs of those who tremble and shiver with fright like the one who knocks on the door of nothingness... And I, I laughed: I was like the spirit of skepticism in that desert. Every billow that swept our unsewn planks dragged a man away—but every billow that roared under my feet seemed to respect me. It was an Ocean like that fiery one, whereinto had fallen the lost angels of Milton, the blind: when they swam past, cutting through the waves, the waters of the swamp of lava parted: death was for the children of God—not for the bastard of evil![30]

"All that night I spent with the captain's wife in my arms. These were terrible

[30] Depictions of hell as a mostly liquid environment, in which demons swim through "fiery waves" appear mostly in Book 1 of Milton's epic *Paradise Lost* (1667). John Milton (1608-1674) became completely blind in 1652.

hymeneals, those consummated between a miscreant and a pale, maddening woman: the connubial bed was the Ocean, the foam from the billows was the silk that carpeted our bed. Amid that concert of howls which went on under our feet, the groans suffocated us: and we rolled embraced—fastened to a cable of the raft—over the planks...

"When dawn came, five of us had remained: me, the captain, his wife, and two sailors...

"For a few days we ate some biscuits soaked in the saltiness of the seawater. Then all the most horrible things happened...

"Why are you turning pale, Solfieri? life is like that. You know that as much as I do. What is man? it's the scum that boils today in the torrent and tomorrow fades: something mad and shifting like the wave, fatal like the tomb! What is existence? In youth it's the kaleidoscope of illusions: one lives on the sap of the future. Then we grow old: when we reach our thirties, and the sweat of agonies has turned our hair gray before its time, and our hopes have withered like our faces, we oscillate between the visionary past and this *tomorrow* of old age, cold and desolate—like a corpse that is bathed before burial! Misery! insanity!"

"Very well! misery and insanity!" interrupted a voice.

The one who had spoken was an old man. His forehead showed signs of balding, and long and deep wrinkles furrowed it— they were the ripples which the wind of old age was digging into the sea of his life… Under thick grizzled eyebrows his brown eyes sparkled, and a thick mustache covered part of his lips. He wore a ragged black waistcoat, and a faded cloak of the same color fell from his shoulders.

"Who are you, old man?" asked the storyteller.

"I was passing by outside: the rain was coming down in buckets: the storm was awful: I entered. Good evening, gentlemen! if there is another cup on your table, fill it to the brim and I shall drink with you."

"Who are you?"

"Who am I? in truth it would be difficult to tell: I've seen much of the world, at each instant changing name and life.—I was a poet—and as a poet I sang. I was a soldier, and bathed my youthful brow in the last sunrays of the eagle of Waterloo.[31]—I shook hands with the man of the century in the heat of the battle. I drank in a tavern with Bocage, the Portuguese; I knelt in front of Dante's tomb in Italy; and I went to Greece to dream

[31] Periphrasis for Napoleon. The "man of the century" in the next sentence also refers to Napoleon.

like Byron in that tomb of glories past.[32]—Who am I? I was a poet at twenty, a libertine at thirty; at forty, I am a vagabond without a country or beliefs. I've sat in the shade of every sun, I've kissed the lips of women from all countries: and from all that peregrination I've brought back two memories only—the love of a woman who died in my arms on the first night of drunkenness and fever—and the agony of a poet... From her, I have a withered rose and the ribbon that held her hair. From him—look..."

The old man took out of his pocket a bundle: its wrapping was a red kerchief: they untied it—inside there was a skull.

"A skull!" they cried around; "are you a grave robber?"

"Look, young man, if you understand the science of Gall and Spurzheim,[33] tell me, from the protuberance of this forehead, and

[32] Manuel Maria Barbosa du Bocage (1765-1805) was a Portuguese poet famous for his bohemian life. The grave of Dante (1265-1321) is in Ravenna. Byron (1788-1824) first traveled to Greece ("the tomb of glories past") in 1809-1811. He then left in 1823 to take part in the Greek War of Independence.

[33] The German Franz Joseph Gall (1758-1828) was the founder of phrenology (the pseudoscience, popular especially in the first half of the 19th century, which claimed to identify personality traits from the contours of the human skull). Johann Gaspar Spurzheim (1776-1832), another German, was Gall's assistant and successor.

from the bumps of this head, who might this man have been?"

"Perhaps a poet—perhaps a madman."

"Very well! you have guessed right. Only you were mistaken not to say that perhaps both things at the same time. Seneca said so—poetry is insanity.[34] Perhaps genius is a hallucination, and enthusiasm might need intoxication to write the sanguinary and fervent hymn of Rouget de l'Isle[35] or, in the creation of the dreadful panel of the dead Christ by Holbein, to study the corruption in the corpse.[36] In Dante's mysterious life, in

[34] A reference to a famous passage in the essay *De Tranquillitate Animi* (On the Tranquility of Mind), Part XVII, by Seneca the Younger (4 BC-65 AD). However, Seneca is actually borrowing this idea from Plato, whom he cites as having thought that "the sane mind knocks in vain at the door of poetry," and from Aristotle who had stated that "no great genius has ever existed without some touch of madness."

[35] Claude Joseph Rouget de Lisle (1760-1836) is the author of the music and the lyrics of *La Marseillaise*, the national anthem of France between 1795 and 1804, and again since 1879. When Azevedo was writing, the song was better known as the anthem of Revolutionary France.

[36] *The Body of the Dead Christ in the Tomb* (1520-1522) is a painting by Hans Holbein the Younger (c.1497-1543). It is famous for its realism: the body shows signs of early putrefaction and the dimensions of the life-size painting are quite striking (30.5 x 200 cm), giving it the appearance of a mere "panel."

Marlowe's orgies, in Byron's wanderings, there was a shadow of Hamlet's illness:[37] who knows?"

"But what is the point of all this?"

"Didn't you cry out—misery and insanity!—you, souls where perhaps the breath of God bubbled, brains which the divine light of genius illumined, and which wine filled with vapors, and satiety with mockery? Fill the cups to the brim! fill them up and drink; drink to the memory of the brain that burned within this skull, of the soul that dwelt here, of the poet—madman—Werner![38] and I will cry out one more time:—misery and insanity!"

The old man emptied his glass, covered himself and left. Bertram continued his story.

"I was telling you that a horrible thing was going to take place: there was no more food, and within man awakened the voice of instinct, of the hungry entrails, asking for their food like the dog of the slaughterhouse, looking for blood.

"Hunger! thirst!... the most horrible thing that is...

[37] Dante (1265-1321) spent the last two decades of his life in exile and there is much speculation about his European travels. The Elizabethan playwright Christopher Marlowe (1564-1593) is alleged to have been a spy and is notorious for his drinking and sexual encounters. Byron (see also note 32) traveled widely through Europe and the Mediterranean. Hamlet's "illness" is madness.

[38] Werner is the protagonist of Byron's eponymous Gothic play, first published in 1822.

"In truth, gentlemen, man is a perfect creature! A sublime sculptor, God exhausted all of his refinement in the chiseling of that marble. Divine Prometheus filled his protuberant cranium with the light of genius. He raised him by the hand, showed him the world from the mountaintop, as Satan four centuries later did to Christ,[39] and said to him: See; all this is beautiful—vales and hills, seawater foaming, forest leaves trembling and rustling like the wings of my angels—all this is yours. I made the world beautiful for you in the purple veil of twilight, I gilded it for you in the rays of my face. Behold, king of the earth! bathe your Olympian brow in these breezes, in this dew, in the foam of these waterfalls. Dream like the night, sing like the angels, sleep among the flowers! Look! amid the florid leaves of the valley sleeps a creature, as white as the veil of my virgins, as fair as the reflection of my clouds, as harmonious as the zephyrs of the sky through the groves of the earth.—She is yours: awaken her: love her, and she shall love you; in her bosom, in the waves of that hair, drown yourself like the sun amid mists. King in her breast, king on earth, live on love and faith, on poetry and beauty, arise, go and you shall be happy!

[39] The timeline here could make sense if Azevedo refers to Aeschylus's *Prometheia* trilogy (written around 430 BC).

"All this is beautiful, yes; but it's the bitterest irony, the most arid disappointment of all ironies and of all disappointments. All this fades before two rather prosaic facts—hunger and thirst.

"The genius, the lofty eagle which is lost in the clouds, which warms itself in the effluvium of the most ardent sunlight—to fall, thus, with sordid and verminous wings into the mud of the moors? Poet, why, in the middle of the most sublime rapture of the spirit, does a sarcastic and Mephistophelian voice shout to you—my Faust, illusions! reality is matter: God wrote Ἀνάγκη—on his creature's forehead.[40]—Don Juan! why do you weep for this lukewarm kiss by Haidée who faints in your arms?[41] the prostitute will sell you more burning ones tomorrow!... Misery!... And to say that all that is most divine in man, most saintly and fragrant in the soul, is infused into the mud of reality, is stirred in the quagmire and still finds an infamous convulsion to say—I am happy!...

[40] Ananke (Ἀνάγκη) is an Ancient Greek personification of Destiny (the term is also translated as inevitability or necessity). Goethe mentions it explicitly in his poetry and implicitly in his masterpiece *Faust*, in which Heinrich Faust is seduced by Mephistopheles's argument that spiritual things are illusory, unlike worldly pursuits.

[41] Haidée is a major character in Byron's *Don Juan*. She is a pirate's daughter who falls in love with Don Juan and dies of a broken heart when her father enslaves her lover and takes him to Constantinople.

"All this, gentlemen, to tell you a very simple thing... an old and worn-out fact—a practice of the sea, a law of shipwreck—anthropophagy.

"Two days after the food ran out three people remained: myself, the captain, and her—three figures as emaciated as corpses, whose bare chests panted with agony, whose sunken, somber eyes were bloodshot with madness.

"The custom of the sea—I don't mean the voice of physical nature, the cry of man's selfishness—commands the death of one for the life of all. We drew lots—the captain was bound to die.

"Then, the instinct for life awakened in him. For one day more of existence, one day more of hunger and thirst, of bed wet and swept by the cold northern winds, some dead hours more of blasphemies and agonies, of hope and despair—of prayers and incredulity—of fever and anxiety—the man knelt, wept, groaned at my feet...

"'Look,' said the wretch, 'let's wait until tomorrow... God shall have mercy on us... By your mother, by your mother's womb! by God, if he exists! let me, let me still live!'

"Oh! Hope is like a parasite that bites and tears through the trunk, but when the latter falls, when it dies and rots, it still clings to it with its convulsive arms! Wait! when the sea

51

wind lashes the waves, when the foam of the ocean washes your livid and naked body, when the horizon is empty and boundless, and the sails that gleam white in the distance seem to flee! Poor lunatic!

"I laughed at the old man.—My entrails were on fire.—To die today, tomorrow, or the day after—it was all indifferent to me, but that day I was hungry, and I laughed because I was hungry.

"The old man reminded me that he had taken me aboard, that he had had mercy on me—he reminded me that he had loved me— and a torrent of sobs and tears choked the brave man who had never paled before death.

"It seems that death in the ocean is terrible to other men: when their faces are spattered with blood and their hands are soaked in it, they run towards death like a river to the sea—like the rattlesnake to fire. But here—in the desert—in the waters—they dread it, they tremble before that cold skull of death!

"I laughed because I was hungry.

"Then the man stood up. Fury had awakened in him—with the last agony. He was faltering, and a cold sweat ran down his emaciated chest. He held me tight into his ashen arms, and we fought hand to hand, chest to chest, foot to foot—for one day of misery!

"The yellowish moon raised its faded face, like a harlot weary with a night of depravity: the dark sky seemed to mock the two dying men fighting for one hour of agony…

"The valiant fighter became unsteady—he fell—I put my foot on his throat—I choked him—and he expired…

"Don't you cover your faces with your hands—you would do just the same… That corpse was our food for two days…

"Then the seabirds were already coming down to share my prey; and in my queasy nights a shadow came to claim its ration of human meat…

"I threw the rest into the sea…

"The captain's wife and I spent—one day, two days—without eating or drinking…

"Then she proposed to die with me.—I said yes. That day was the last gasp of the love that had burned us—we wasted it in convulsions so as to still feel the fresh honey of voluptuousness bathe our lips… It was the feverish joy which two creatures can have in the delirium of death. When I got loose from her arms her weakness made her hallucinate. Her delirium grew longer, longer: she leaned forward over the waves and drank the salty water, and she offered it to me with her wan hands, saying it was wine. The cold cackle came rather in a hurry…

"She was insane.

"I didn't sleep—I couldn't sleep: a burning drowsiness consumed my eyelids: the breath in my chest seemed fire: my dry, cracked lips were only bedewed by blood.

"I had a fever in the brain—and my stomach was hungry. I was hungry like a beast.

"I held her tightly in my arms, I pressed on her lips my mouth on fire: I squeezed her convulsively—I suffocated her. She was still so beautiful!

"I don't know what strange delirium took possession of me. A vertigo surrounded me. The sea seemed to laugh at me, and it span around, foaming and greenish, like a whirlpool. The clouds hovered, running about, and seemed to filter black blood. The wind that passed through my hair whispered a memory...

"Suddenly I felt alone. A wave had snatched the corpse from me. I saw her floating, as pale as her white clothes, half-naked, with her hair bathed with water: I saw her emerging in the foam of the billows, disappearing, and floating again: then I could no longer distinguish her—she was like the foam of the billows, like a sheet thrown into the waters...

"How many hours, how many days I spent in that drowsiness, I don't even know... When I awoke from that nightmare of a sleepless man, I was aboard a ship.

"It was the English brig[42] *Swallow* that saved me...

"Hey, tavernkeeper, you bastard of Satan! don't you see I'm thirsty, and the bottles are dry, as dry as your cheeks and as our throats?"

[42] A brig is a vessel with two masts and square rigs. There was a brig-sloop (a small warship with two masts) called HMS *Swallow* (launched in 1805 and decommissioned in 1815), which took part in the Napoleonic Wars.

# IV

## Gennaro

Meurs ou tue…
CORNEILLE.[43]

---

[43] French for "Die or kill." A famous line from *Le Cid* (1636), the masterpiece of French playwright Pierre Corneille (1606-1684). It belongs to Don Diègue, the hero's father, and it refers to the duty of avenging one's honor.

"Gennaro, are you sleeping, or are you savoring the taste of the last sip of wine, of the last puff from your pipe?"

"No: while you were telling your story, I remembered a leaf of life, a dry and reddened leaf as the autumn's, swept away by the wind."

"A story?"

"Yes: it's one of my stories: you know, Bertram, I'm a painter; it's a sad memory the one I'm about to reveal, because it's the story of an old man and two women, as beautiful as two visions of light.

"Godofredo Walsh was one of those sublime old men, on whose heads the gray hair resembles the silver diadem of genius. Already old, he had married in second nuptials a twenty-year-old beauty. Godofredo was a painter: some said that this marriage had been an artistic love for that Roman beauty, as if made in the mold of ancient beauties—others believed it was compassion for the poor girl who made a living as a model. The fact is that he wanted her as a daughter—like Laura, the only daughter from his first marriage—Laura, ruddy like a rose, and blond like an angel.

"Back then I was a young man: I was an apprentice painter at Godofredo's house. I was handsome, then; for thirty years have passed, for my hair and face had not faded yet, as in these long forty-two years of life! I was that type of lad still pure, exuding artlessness, pensive and melancholy as Raphael portrayed himself in the painting at the Barberini Gallery.[44] I was almost the age of the master's wife.—Nauza was twenty, and I was eighteen years old.[45]

"I loved her, but my love was as pure as my dreams of an eighteen-year-old. Nauza also loved me: it was such a pure feeling! it was a solitary and balmy emotion, like the springs filled with flowers and with gentle winds which rocked us to sleep under the skies of Italy.

"As I said—the master had a daughter named Laura. She was a pale girl, with chestnut brown hair and bluish eyes; her complexion was white, only that sometimes, when shyness incensed her, two roses reddened her face and stood out against the marble background. Laura seemed to want me as a brother. Her laughter, her fifteen-year-old girl's kisses were solely for me. At night, when I went to bed,

[44] Raphael's *Self-Portrait* (c.1504-1506) mentioned here was painted in Florence and is now in the Uffizi Gallery. The Palazzo Barberini (in Rome) houses *La Fornarina*, the portrait of a young woman, painted by Raphael in 1518-1519.

[45] Gennaro's sense of the passage of time is dubious here. He might have meant "forty-eight years" a couple of lines above.

as I passed through the dark hallway with my lamp, a shadow would extinguish its light and a kiss would be laid on my face, in the darkness.

"Many nights, it was so.

"One morning—I was still sleeping—the master had left and Nauza had gone to church—when Laura came into my bedroom and closed the door: she lay by my side. I woke up in her embraces.

"The fire of my eighteen years, the virginal spring of a beauty, still innocent, the half-naked breast of a maiden pressing against mine: all this, as I awakened from the candid dreams of dawn, drove me insane...

"Every morning Laura came to my bedroom...

"Three months passed like this. One day she came into my room and said to me:

"'Gennaro, I am dishonored forever... At first I wanted to delude myself; I cannot any longer—I am with child...'

"A lightning bolt striking by my feet would not have frightened me that much.

"'It is urgent that you marry me, that you ask my father for my hand, do you hear me, Gennaro?'

"I remained silent.

"'Don't you love me, then?'

"I still remained silent.

"'Oh! Gennaro! Gennaro!'

"And she fell upon my shoulder, ravaged by sobs. I carried her thus, cold and distraught, to her room.

"She never spoke to me of marriage again.

"What was I to do? tell her father everything, and ask for her hand in marriage? It would have been madness; he would have killed me and her: or at least throw me out of his house... And Nauza? I loved her more and more each day. It was a terrible struggle between duty and love, and between duty and remorse.

"Laura never spoke to me again. Her smile was cold: she grew paler every day; but the pregnancy was not progressing, indeed no sign of it was noticeable...

"The old man spent the nights wandering in the dark. He no longer painted. Seeing his daughter dying to the secret sounds of a deathly harmony, growing ever paler, the wretched man tore out his gray hair.

"I, however, had not forgotten Nauza, nor had she forgotten me. My love was ever the same: there were always nights of hope and thirst which bathed my pillow with tears. Only sometimes did the shadow of remorse cross my mind; but her image dissipated all those mists...

"One night... it was horrible... I was sent for; Laura was dying. In her fever she murmured my name and words that nobody could retain; so rushed and confused they sounded. I entered her room: the sick girl recognized me. She rose, white, her face wet with copious sweat: she called me. I sat by her bedside. She held my hand tight in her cold hands and whispered in my ears:

"'Gennaro, I forgive you: I forgive you for everything... You were despicable... I'm dying... I've been a fool... I'm dying... because of you... your son... mine... I will see him again... but in Heaven... my son whom I killed... before he was born...'

"She let out a scream: she convulsively stretched her arms as if to repel an idea, rubbed her hand over her lips as if to wipe away the last drops of a drink, twisted on her bed, livid, cold, bathed in icy sweat, and gasped... It was her last breath.

"A whole year passed like this for me. The old man seemed to have gone mad. Every night he locked himself in the room where Laura had died: there he spent the whole night in solitude. Did he sleep? not at all! For long hours I listened to him panting with anxiety, other times choking with sobs. Then everything hushed: the silence lasted for hours: the room was dark: and then the master's heavy strides were heard across the room, though swaying like those of a staggering drunkard.

"One night I told Nauza I loved her: I knelt beside her, kissed her hands, showered her lap with tears: she turned her face from me: I believed it was disdain, I stood up.

"'So, Nauza, you don't love me,' I said.

"She kept her face turned away.

"'Farewell, then: forgive me if I have offended you: my love is folly, my life is despair—what am I left to do? Farewell, I will go far, far away from here... perhaps then I shall be able to weep without remorse...'

"I took her hand and kissed it.

"She left her hand on my lips.

"When I raised my head, I saw her: she had burst into tears.

"'Nauza! Nauza! one word, do you love me?'

. . . . . . . . . . . . . . . . . . . . . . . . . . . . . . . . . . . .
. . . . . . . . . . . . . . . . . . . . . . . . . . . . . . . . . . . .

"Everything else was a dream: the moon passed through the panes of an open window and shone upon her: I had never seen her so pure and divine!

. . . . . . . . . . . . . . . . . . . . . . . . . . . . . . . . . . . .
. . . . . . . . . . . . . . . . . . . . . . . . . . . . . . . . . . . .

"And the nights the master spent sobbing by the empty bed of his daughter, I spent in his bed, in Nauza's arms.

"One night something astonishing happened.

"The master came to Nauza's bed. It groaned and wept, that cavernous, husky voice: he took me by the arm with force, awoke me, and dragged me to Laura's room…

"He threw me to the floor: he closed the door. A lamp was lit in the bedroom, in front of a canvas board. He lifted the sheet that covered it.—It was of the dying Laura. And of me, as pale as her, trembling like one condemned. The girl with pale lips was whispering in my ear…

"I trembled to see my semblance, so livid, on the canvas: and I remembered that on that day, as I left the dead girl's bedroom, in her mirror, which was still hanging by the window, I had been horrified to see myself cadaverous…

"A tremor, a chill, seized me. I knelt and shed burning tears. I confessed everything: it seemed to me that it was she who commanded it, that it was Laura risen from the sheets of her bed, who had ignited my remorse, and the remorse tore at my heart.

"By God! what agony that was!

"The next day the master spoke to me coldly. He lamented the loss of his daughter; though without a tear. But as for what had passed during the night, not a word.

"Every night was the same torture, every day the same coldness.

"The master was a somnambulist...

"And so I did not believe myself lost...

"Nevertheless, I remembered that one night, as I was leaving Laura's room with the master, I saw in the dark a white garment pass me by, some loose hair grazed me, and on the slabs of the hallway some timid steps of bare feet snapped... It was Nauza who had seen everything and heard everything, who had woken and missed me in bed, who had heard those sobs and groans, and had run to see...

. . . . . . . . . . . . . . . . . . . . . . . . . . . . . . . . . . . .
. . . . . . . . . . . . . . . . . . . . . . . . . . . . . . . . . . .

"One night, after supper, Master Walsh took his cape and a lantern, and summoned me to accompany him. He had to get out of the town and did not want to go alone. We left together: the night was dark and cold. Autumn had stripped the trees of their leaves and the first breaths of winter rustled in the dry leaves on the ground. We walked along for a long time: the farther we ventured into the mountains, the more solitary the path was. The old man stopped. It was by the foot of a mountain. To the right the rock opened into a trail; to the left the stones, loosened by our feet at each stride, were detached and rolled down the precipice, and an instant later a sound was heard, as of water when a weight falls into it…

"The night was pitch black. Only the lantern illuminated the tortuous path we followed. The old man cast his eyes in the obscurity of the abyss and laughed.

"'Wait for me there,' he said; 'I'll come back at once.'

"Godofredo took the lantern and proceeded to the peak of the mountain: I sat on the path, waiting for him: I saw that light now disappear, now reappear through the trees in the zigzags of the path. Finally I saw it stop. The old man knocked on the door of a cabin: the door opened. He went in. What came to pass in there I know not: when the door opened again, a livid and disheveled woman appeared with a torch in her hand.

"The door closed. Some minutes later the master was with me.

"The old man set down the lantern on a rock, took off his cape, and said to me:

"'Gennaro, I want to tell you a story. It is a crime, and I want you to be its judge. An old man was married to a beautiful young woman. From another marriage he had a daughter, beautiful as well. An apprentice—a wretch whom he had lifted from the dust, as the wind sometimes lifts a leaf, but whom he could reduce to it whenever he wanted…'

67

"I shuddered, as the old man's gaze seemed to wound me.

"'Never have you heard this story, my good Gennaro?'

"'Never,' said I with difficulty and trembling.

"'Well then: that despicable man dishonored the poor old man—betrayed him like Judas betrayed Jesus.'

"'Master, I'm sorry!'

"'Sorry! and was the wicked one sorry for the old man's poor heart?'

"'Have pity!'

"'And did he take pity on the dishonored infanticidal virgin?'

"'Ah!' I cried.

"'What is it? do you know this criminal?'

"His scornful voice stifled me.

"'You see then, Gennaro,' he said, changing his tone: 'if there were a punishment worse than death, I would inflict it upon you. Look at this precipice! It's dreadful! if you saw it in the daytime, your eyes would darken, and down there you might roll—from vertigo! It's a safe tomb: and it will keep the secret, like a breast keeps the dagger. Only the crows will go there to see you; only the crows and the worms. And so, if you still have any remorse in your cursed heart, say your last prayer; but be brief: the executioner awaits the victim: the hyena is hungry for the corpse...'

"There I was, hanging close to death. I only had the choice of suicide or being murdered. Killing the old man was impossible. A fight between me and him would have been insane. He was robust, his stature tall, his muscular arms would have broken me like the gale bursts a dry branch. Besides, he was armed. I—I was a feeble child: at my first step, he would have hurled me off the rock on whose edge I stood… the only thing left was dying with him, dragging him with me in my fall.—But what for?

"I bent over the abyss: everything was black: the wind groaned down there, in the bare branches, in the heather, in the parched brambles, and the torrent rattled on the bottom, foaming on the rocks.

"I was afraid.

"Prayers, threats, all was in vain.

"'I'm ready,' I said.

"The old man laughed: infernal was that laugh from his fever-cracked lips. I only saw that laughter… Then came the vertigo… the suffocating air, a weight dragging me down, like those nightmares in which one falls from a tower and still holds on fast by a hand, but the hand wearies, weakens, sweats, chills… It was horrible: branch after branch, leaf by leaf, the bushes snapped in my hands: the dried roots which came out down the precipice snapped under my weight, and my chest bled amid the brambles. The fall was very swift... suddenly I felt nothing more... When I awoke I was by a peasant's cabin where they had picked me up by the torrent, caught in the branches of a gigantic holm oak which shaded the river.

"It was after a day and a night of delirium that I awoke. As soon as I recovered, an idea came to me: to go see the master. Seeing me thus saved from that horrible death, perhaps he would take pity on me, forgive me, and then I would be his slave, his dog, anything that is most abject in a man who humiliates himself—anything!—if only he forgave me. Living with that remorse seemed impossible to me. So I left: on the path I found a dagger. I picked it up: it was the master's. Then an idea of vengeance and insolence came to me. He had wanted to kill me, he had laughed at my agony, and I was to go cry at his feet only for him to reject me again, to spit in my face, and tomorrow to seek another, more certain revenge? Humiliate myself, I, when he had slain me! My hair stood on end, and cold sweat rolled down my face.

"When I arrived at the master's house I found it locked. I knocked—no one opened. The garden of the house gave out onto the street: I jumped over the wall: everything was deserted and the back doors were locked as well. One of them was weak: with a little effort I broke it open. To the clatter of the

70

door that fell, only the echo responded in the rooms. All windows were shut: and yet it was a clear day outside. Everything was dark: not even one lamp was lit. I groped my way up to the painter's room. I arrived there: I opened the windows and the daylight poured into the empty room. I came then to Nauza's room; I opened the door and a pestilent waft ran out of there. A ray of light fell on a table.—Next to it was a woman's form with the face on the table, her hair falling down: thrown onto an armchair was a figure covered with a cloak. Between them was a glass where a powdery residue had settled. Near it was an empty flask. Later I learned—the old woman from the cabin was someone who sold poison: it had to be, since the white powder in the glass seemed to be poison...

"I lifted the woman's hair, raised her head... It was Nauza, but Nauza the corpse, already faded by decay. It was no longer that whitest statue, with smooth cheeks and the neck of snow... it was a yellowish corpse... I lifted one end of the other's cape—the body fell prostrate, with the head down; the snap of the skull echoed on the pavement... It was the old man—dead as well, purple and rotten: I saw him—from his mouth ran a greenish foam." . . . . . . . . . . . . . . . . . . . . . . . . . . . . .
. . . . . . . . . . . . . . . . . . . . . . . . . . . . . . . . . . . .
. . . . . . . . . . . . . . . . . . . . . . . . . . . . . . . . . .

# V

## Claudius Hermann

... Extacy!
My pulse as yours doth temperately keep time
And makes a healthful music: It is no madness
That I have utter'd.
SHAKESPEARE,
HAMLET.[46]

---

[46] "Ecstasy!/ My pulse, as yours, doth temperately keep
time,/ And makes as healthful music: It is not madness,/
That I have utter'd" (Act III, scene iv). This is Hamlet
answering the queen, trying to convince her that the ghost
of his dead father, whom he keeps seeing, is not "the very
coinage of [his] brain."

"And you, Hermann! Your time has come. One by one we have evoked a corpse from the cemetery of the past. One by one we have lifted its shroud to show a stain of blood. Speak, for your time has come."

"Claudius fancies some sonnet in the fashion of Petrarch, some halo of purity like that of the pure spirits from *The Messiah*!"[47] said Johann between a smoke and a chuckle, raising his head from the table.

"Well then! do you want a story? I could tell, like you, follies from nights of orgy; but what for? It had been out of scorn that Faust went reminding Mephistopheles the hours of perdition he had dealt with him. You know all those clouds from my past, you have read abundantly the faded book of my libertine existence. If you don't remember them, the first woman of the streets could tell them. In this dark torrent called life, which flows towards the past while we walk towards the future, I have shed many a belief and cast

[47] *Der Messias* (1748-1773) is a religious epic poem by Friedrich Gottlieb Klopstock (1724-1803), extremely popular in the 18th century. The first canto focuses on Gabriel the Archangel's trip through heaven. Petrarch or Francesco Petrarca (1304-1374) is famous for *Il Canzoniere*, a collection (mostly) of sonnets on the theme of courtly love.

away my most fragrant garments to don the tunic of the Saturnalia![48] The past is what has been, it is the flower which has withered, the sun which has extinguished: the cadaver which has putrefied. Tears for it? it would be madness! Let it sleep with its dark memories! let only the opened forget-me-nots be revived, be awakened in that swamp! let the effluvium of some pure memory overflood that non-being!"

"Bravo! Bravissimo! Claudius, you're completely drunk! truly, you're a romantic!"

"Silence, Bertram! certainly this is not a legend to be inscribed after those of yours: one of those things which are told with elbows on the red tablecloth, and lips drizzled with wine and satiated with kisses... But what matters?

"All of you who love gambling, who saw one day a wave of gold rushing down that abyss, whirling down to its bottom, like a sea of hopes crashing against the fickleness of chance, you know very well what vertigo then overwhelms us: you can better conceive the madness which deliriously drives us to those games of thousands of men, where fortunes, aspirations, life itself vanish in the swiftness

[48] Saturnalia was a major holiday and carnival in ancient Rome. In modern times, the word was often used as synonymous with any kind of unrestrained revelry or orgy.

of a race, where all that complex of miseries and desires, of crimes and virtues which is called existence is gambled away on a team of horses!

"I used to bet like a man who can't be hurt by becoming a pauper: one can get replete with luxury, and that is a terrible kind of glut! nothing is enough for it: neither dances from the Orient, nor the Roman Lupercalia, nor the burning of an entire city[49] would feed its vim of death, that *vitality of poison*—of which Byron speaks.[50] My bet on the *turf* was my entire fortune.[51] I was rich, very rich then: in London, nobody was more ostentatious with lavish debauchery: no nabob squandered in one night the sums that I did. I poured the sweat of three generations onto the beds of courtesans, and over the floor of my orgies.

"The moment the races were about to begin, when everyone felt feverish with

[49] The Lupercalia was a Roman holiday (15 February), marked by fertility rituals. In the 18th and 19th centuries it was erroneously associated with a lottery scheme in which people were paired up for sex. The burning of a city is likely a reference to the Great Fire of Rome (64 A.D.), often implausibly attributed to Emperor Nero's desire to clear land for his own palace.

[50] From *Childe Harold's Pilgrimage* (Canto III, xxiv). The original has the phrase in italics, but in Portuguese (*vitalidade do veneno*).

[51] *Turf* (in English and in italics in the original) has become "turfe" in contemporary Portuguese. Borrowed from English, the term refers to the racetrack.

impatience—a murmur ran through the crowds—a smile—and then it was the brows that broadened—and then a woman passed by on horseback.

"Had you seen her as I did—on the black horse, in velvet clothes, with vivid cheeks, her gaze burning under the disdain of her eyelashes, a queen translucent in all that superb demeanor: had you seen her, so beautiful with her plastic and harmonious beauty, lovely in her pure and satiny colors, with black hair, and the white complexion of her brow; the oval of the flushed cheeks, the fire of mother-of-pearl on the thin lips, the elegance of the neck, standing out in the outfit of an Amazon: had you seen her thus, in faith, gentlemen, you would not laugh out with scorn as you laugh now!"

"Romanticism! you must be very drunk, Claudius, that despite your dry lips like Lovelace's, and your insensibility like Don Juan's,[52] poetry might still come to bear you a kiss!"

"Laugh, yes! you wretches! who don't comprehend what fire might burn on those

[52] Both Lovelace (a character in Samuel Richardson's 1748 novel *Clarissa*) and Don Juan (whose legend began with a 1630 play by Tirso de Molina) are fictional libertines. Don Juan's name is spelled here (and again in one of the following lines) "D. Juan" and not in italics, to show it is not a reference to Byron's poem (see notes 29 and 41).

lips of Lovelace's, and how love does gasp under the rain-dripping clothes of Don Juan the libertine! You insane, who have never dreamed of Lovelace without his mask, perhaps weeping for Clarisse Harlowe, poor angel, whose white wings he would wither... cursing that fatality which turns love into infamy and crime! A thousand times insane that you have never dreamed of the Spaniard waking at the lupanar, passing his hand over his brow, and roaring with remorse and longing as he remembers so many pure visions of the past!"

"Bravo! bravo!"

"Poetry! poetry!" murmured Bertram.

"Poetry! why utter its name, holy as a mystery, to the chaste virgin, in the dark mire of the tavern? Why should the star of love remind her of it by the lamplight of debauchery? Poetry! know you what poetry is?"

"Half a hundred sonorous and vain words which a handful of pale men understand, a scale of sounds and harmonies which to those foolish souls seem like ideas, and awaken illusions in them like the moon awakens shadows... This is what is called poets. Now, in the ideal, in woman, the aftertaste of the latest romance, the delirium and the passion of the latest heroine of a novelette, and the uncertain and vague present of a mystical pleasure, by which the virgin dies of voluptuousness, without knowing why…"

"Silence, Bertram! your brain has been burned by wine, like volcanic lava burns the grass and flowers of the meadow. Silence! you are like those plants which grow and sink into the dead sea: a calcareous crystallization covers them, they stunt and wither. Poetry, I will tell you in turn, is the flight of morning birds in the warm bath of the red clouds of dawn, it is the deer that rolls on the dew of the grassy mountain, forgetting tomorrow's death, yesterday's agony on its bed of flowers!"

"Enough, Claudius: for what you there say nobody understands: it's words, words, words, as Hamlet has said[53]: and all this is inane and vacuous like a dry skull, deceitful like the foul vapors of the earth which the sun at twilight iridizes with a thousand colors, and which are called clouds, or like that mocking, nebulous fairy called poetry!"

"To the story! to the story! Claudius— can't you see that this conversation makes us yawn with boredom?"

"Well then: I shall tell the rest of the story:—By the end of that day I had doubled my fortune.

[53] In *Hamlet* (II, ii). To Polonius's question, "What do you read my lord?" Hamlet answers "Words, words, words."

"On the following day I saw her: it was at the theater. I don't know what was being performed; I don't know what I was listening to, nor what I was watching: I just know that a woman was there—beautiful as everything that passes most purely through the conception of the sculptor. That woman was Duchess Eleonora... The following day I saw her at a ball... Then... It would be too long to tell you: six months! can you conceive that? six months of agony and yearning desire—six months of love with the thirst of a beast! six months! how long they were!

"One day I thought it was too much. All that time had been spent in contemplation— in seeing her, loving her, and dreaming of her: I held my hands tight, swearing that this would go no further, that it was too much waiting in vain: and that if she should not come like Gulnare at the feet of the Corsair,[54] it behooved him to go meet her.

"One night all was asleep in the Duke's palace. The Duchess, tired from the ball, fell asleep on a divan. The golden light from the alabaster lamp flickered on her pale forehead. She looked like a fairy sleeping in the moonlight...

[54] In Byron's *The Corsair* (1814), Gulnare comes to Conrad's cell to help him escape after he had failed to free her and the women in the pacha's harem.

"The curtain in the room stirred: a man stood there—absorbed. His head was hot and febrile and he rested it on the doorway.

"Weakness was cowardly: and besides, that man had bought a key and an hour from the venal infamy of a servant; that man had sworn that he would enjoy that woman on that night: had it been poison he still would have drunk the honey of that flower, the scarlet liquor from that cup. As for those prejudices of honor and adultery, don't you laugh at them—not that he laughed at them. He loved, and he desired: his will was like the blade of a dagger—to wound or to shatter.

"On the table there were a glass and a flagon of wine: he filled the glass: it was Spanish wine… He came close to her, lifted her with her velvet clothes untied, her hair somewhat loose still intermingled with precious stones and flowers, her breasts half-naked, where diamonds glittered like drops of dew; he lifted her in his arms; he gave her a kiss. With the warmth of that kiss, half-naked, she awoke: amid her vague dreams an illusion was fading perhaps; she murmured 'love!' and with half-open eyes let her head drop and she fell asleep again.

"The man took a small emerald vial out of his bosom. He brought it to her half-open lips: he poured a few drops that she absorbed without feeling them. He laid her down and waited. Shortly thereafter she was most profoundly asleep... The beverage was a narcotic mixed with a few drops of those stimulating liquors which awaken fever in one's cheeks and voluptuous desire in one's bosom.

"The man was down on his knees: his chest trembled, and he was pale as after a long sensual night. Everything seemed to tremble around him... She was naked: neither velvet nor light veil concealed her. The man rose, pushed aside the curtain.

"The lamp shone brighter—and went out...

"The man was Claudius Hermann. . . . . . .
. . . . . . . . . . . . . . . . . . . . . . . . . . . . . . . . . . . . .
. . . . . . . . . . . . . . . . . . . . . . . . . . . . . . . . . .

"When I got up, I wrapped myself in my cloak and went out in the streets. I wanted to make for my palace; but I was as dizzy as a drunkard. I staggered and the ground was as slippery as to one who faints. One idea, nevertheless, haunted me.—After that woman, there would be nothing left for me. Whoever has once drunk the juice of the purple grapes of paradise must never again get drunk with the nectar of the earth... When the honey ran out, what would remain but suicide?

"One week passed thus: every night I drank from the lips of the sleeper one century of pleasure. One month! the month in which the balls of the Carnival went on deliriously, in which she fell asleep feverishly with her cheeks on fire!

"One night—it was after a ball—I waited for her in the alcove, hidden behind her bed. — Into the glass filled with water that was by the bedside I had poured the last drops of the philter, when she entered with the Duke.

"Such handsome youth was he! Before he left her, he ran both hands over her temples and gave her a kiss. Enraptured by that kiss, the angel leaned her head on his shoulder and enlaced him with her bare arms, gleaming with her jeweled bracelets. The Duke was thirsty, he reached for the Duchess's glass, sipped a few drops; she took the glass from him, she drank the rest. I saw them thus: that husband still so young, that woman—ah! so beautiful!... of a still virgin complexion—and I held the dagger tight...

"'Will you come today, Maffio?' said she.

"'Yes, my soul.'

"A kiss rustled and drowned the two souls. And I in the shadow smiled; because I knew he would not come.

. . . . . . . . . . . . . . . . . . . . . . . . . . . . . . . . . . . . . .
. . . . . . . . . . . . . . . . . . . . . . . . . . . . . . . . . . . .

"He left: she started to undress. I saw the glittering clothes, the flowers, and the jewels drop one by one, her lustrous black braids unravel—and then she appeared in the white veil of her transparent robe like the statues of half naked nymphs with forms delineated by the tunic drenched in bathwater.

"What I saw—was what I had dreamed of and much more, what you all, poor fools, once imagined as the vision of love upon the body of the harlot! It was the snow-white and blue-veined breasts, tremulous with desire, the head lost amid the rain of black hairs, the lips panting, the whole body palpitating—it was the languidness of disarray, when the body of beauty is most filled with beauty, and as a rose which unfolds wet with dew, the more expanded it is, the more patent is its color.

"The narcotic was most strong: a feverish eagerness parted her lips, exhausted and languid, prostrate on the bed, with pale eyelids, her arms loose and powerless—she seemed to be kissing a shadow.

. . . . . . . . . . . . . . . . . . . . . . . . . . . . . . . . . . . . .
. . . . . . . . . . . . . . . . . . . . . . . . . . . . . . . . . .

"I lifted her from the bed: I carried her in her diaphanous clothes, her satiny form, her loose hair still wet with perfume, her breasts still warm...

"I ran with her through the deserted hallways: I passed through the patio—the last door was closed: I opened it.

"In the street there was a stagecoach: the horses neighed and foamed with impatience.

I got with her inside the carriage.—We departed.

"It was time. One hour later it was dawning.

"Shortly we were out of town.

"There came dawn with its vapors, its rose gardens sprinkled with dew, its velvety clouds and its waters speckled with gold and ruddiness. Nature blushed at the first kiss of the sun, like a fair damsel at the first kiss of the fiancé: not like a mistress weary of a voluptuous night as paganism has painted her; rather like a virgin awakened from her childish dream, half-kneeling before God, praying and murmuring her soothing prayers to the sky that turns blue, to the earth that scintillates, to the waters that turn golden. That dawn descended upon the earth like the breath of God: and amid that light and that fresh air the Duchess slept—pale like the sleep of those mystical creatures from the illuminated manuscripts of the Middle Ages—as beautiful as Titian's sleeping Venus, and as voluptuous as one of Veronese's concubines.[55]

[55] The *Sleeping Venus* is a famous painting of the Italian Renaissance, though it is still unclear if it is the work of Giorgione (c.1478-1510) finished after his death by Titian (1488/1490-1576) or if it is entirely the work of Titian. The second reference is likely to the first scenes of *The Allegory of Love* (1570), a series of four paintings by Paolo Veronese (1528-1588). Veronese, Titian and Tintoretto are usually seen as the three greatest painters of 16th-century Italian Renaissance.

"I kissed her: I felt life evaporating from me and onto her lips. She startled—slightly opened her eyes; but the burden of sleep still overwhelmed her, and her discolored eyelids closed…

"The carriage ever ran.

. . . . . . . . . . . . . . . . . . . . . . . . . . . . . . . . . . . .
. . . . . . . . . . . . . . . . . . . . . . . . . . . . . . . . . .

"The sun was high in the sky—it was midday: the heat was stifling: drops of sweat rolled down the Duchess's forehead, cheeks, and neck, like pearls from a broken necklace… We stopped at an inn: I threw a veil on her face, took her in my arms, and carried her to a room.

"She must have been very beautiful, thus! the servants stopped in the hallways: it was awe at such beauty, rather than indiscreet curiosity.

"The lady of the house came to me.

"'Sir, your wife or sister, whoever she is, shall certainly need a servant to attend her…'

"'Leave me alone: she is asleep.'

"That was my only answer.

"I laid her on the bed: I pulled the curtains, closed the windows so that the light would not disturb her sleep. There was nobody there to see us: we were alone, the man and his angel, and the creature of the earth knelt by the bed of the creature of heaven.

"I don't know how much time passed like this: I don't know whether I slept, but I know that I dreamt of much love and much hope: I don't know whether I was awake, but I saw her ever there, I contemplated each graceful movement of her sleep: I shuddered at each breath which made her breasts shiver, and everything seemed a dream to me—one of those dreams in which the soul abandons itself like a swan, which drowses, to the tune of the waves… I don't know how much time passed like this: I only know that my slumber was broken: the Duchess was sitting on the bed: with her bare arms she was brushing aside the waves of loose hair which covered her face and neck.

"'Is it a dream?' she murmured. 'Where am I? who is this man leaning against my bed?'

"The man did not respond.

"She got out of bed: her first impulse was modesty: she wanted to cover her breasts, which were throbbing with fright, with her little hands. She felt almost naked, exposed to the gaze of a stranger—and she trembled as the poets tell Diana trembled when she saw herself exposed, in her bath, naked, to the gaze of Acteon.[56]

"'Sir, tell me, for pity's sake, if all this is not an illusion… if it is not an infamy! I don't want to even think of it. Maffio shouldn't be long, shouldn't he? my Maffio!... This is all some kind of trickery… But what alcove is this? I had fallen asleep at the palace… how come I have awakened now in a strange room? tell me, is this all Maffio's prank? he wants to laugh at me? But look, look, I tremble, I am afraid.'

"The man did not respond: he had his eyes fixed on that divine form: it would have been the very statue of passion in its pallor, its unwavering gaze, its thirsty lips, if the heaving of the chest had not betrayed its life.

"She knelt down: I do not even know what she was saying. I do not know what words evaporated from those lips: they were perfumes, for the roses from heaven only have perfumes: they were harmonies, for the harps from heaven only have harmonies, and the lip of the beautiful woman is a divine rose, and

[56] In Greek mythology, Acteon or Actaeon was a shepherd who saw Artemis (called Diana by the Romans) bathing in the woods. Artemis cast a spell that would turn him into a stag if he spoke of what he had seen. As Acteon could not keep the secret he was changed into a stag and was torn to pieces by hounds. In a famous Latin version told by the Roman poet Ovid, Acteon was a hunter and was killed by his own hounds after accidentally seeing Diana bathing.

her heart is a harp from heaven. I listened to her, but did not understand her: I only felt that those words were very sweet, that that voice possessed an irresistible talisman for my soul, since only in my childhood dreams, deluded by loves, had such a voice ever reached me. The trills of two virgins embraced in heaven, gilded by the light from the face of God, cleansed by the purest kisses, by the tremulousness of the most palpitating embraces—would not be as sweet!

"The young woman wept, sobbed: finally she stood up.

"I saw her run to the window, she was going to open it... I ran to her and took her by the hands...

"'Well then,' she said, 'I'll scream... if we're not in a desert, if someone passes by here... perhaps they'll rescue me... Help m...'

"I covered her mouth with my hands...

"'Silence, madam!'

"She struggled to free herself from my hands: in the end she felt weak. I let her loose out of pity.

"'Then tell me where I am—tell me, or I'll call for help...'

"'Don't you scream, madam!'

"'Have mercy then and enlighten me then on this apprehension: why all this that I see? All that I think, all that I foresee is quite horrible!'

"'Listen, then,' I said to her. 'There was a woman... she was an angel. There was a man who loved her, as the waters love the moon that silvers them, as the mountain eagles love the sun that gazes at them, that fills them with light and love. I don't even know who he was: he raised himself one day from a life of fever, he forgot it; and he forgot the past, before the transparent eyes of a woman, the stains of his history, in a dawn of joys, where the shadow of that angel was drawn before him... Listen: do not curse him! That man was full of infamy in his past: he had profaned his youth— he had squandered it like the gold butterfly its offspring, casting it into the mud: cold, without beliefs, without hopes, he had stifled one by one his illusions, like an infanticide her children... God had perhaps cursed him! or else he had cursed himself... He had forgotten that he was a man, and that he held within his bosom saintly harmonies like those of the poet... he had forgotten them, and they lay dormant within him in mystery like sighs on the strings of an abandoned guitar. He had forgotten that nature was beautiful, very beautiful indeed, that the bed of flowers at night was fragrant, that the moon was the lamp of love, the breezes of the valley, the perfumes of the poet in his betrothal with the angels, that the dawn had fresh effluviums, and with its virginal clouds, its leaves wet with dew, its misty waters, had enchantments which only the pure souls understand! All this he rejected, forgot... only to remember it stealthily and with scorn in the sweaty hours of debauchery... He was quite contemptible!'

"'But all this does not tell me who you are... nor why I am here...'

"'Listen.—The libertine then loved the angel, turned his face from the past, divested himself of it as of an impure mantle. He tempered himself in the fire of feeling, purified himself with the virginity of that vision, for she was beautiful as a virgin, and reflected that virgin light of the spirit, that brilliance of the divine soul which illuminates forms— which is not from earth, but from heaven. Time had not yet tainted the madman's heart with an incurable leprosy: nor had it engraved an indelible seal on his brow—*impurity*! He abandoned the life he had led, he snubbed his comrades, his venal mistresses, his feverish sleepless nights: he wanted to extinguish all taste for that existence, as the man who has lost an entire fortune in gambling wishes to forget reality.

"'And the man was able to forget all this. But he was still not happy. He spent his nights around her palace: he saw her sometimes lovely and wan in the moonlight, on the deserted terrace, or distinguished her forms in the shadow that passed through the curtains of the open window of her illuminated bedroom. At balls he followed with looks of envy that body which throbbed in the dances. In the theater, amid the rolling waves of harmony, when ecstasy floated in that balsamic and luminous ambiance, he saw nothing but her—and only her! And his hours in bed—not his hours of sleep, for he hardly slept sometimes—were long with impatience and insomnia,—other times short with ardent dreams! The poor madman had one day an idea; it was a dark one, yes, but it was a fateful one. What he did, I do not know: nor will you ever know. And then drunk enough to dream of you, mad enough in the fiery dreams of his delirium to imagine enjoying you, he was profane enough to steal from a temple the ciborium of the purest gold.—That man—have mercy on him, for he will love you on his knees… Oh angel, Eleonora…'

"'My God! my God! why so much infamy, so much mud upon me? Oh! my Madonna! why have you cursed my life, why have you let so black a stain fall upon my head?'

"The tears, the sobs stifled her voice.

"'Forgive me, madam, here I am at your feet! have pity on me, for I have suffered much, for I have loved you, for I love you so! Compassion! for I shall be your slave: I

93

shall kiss the soles of your feet; I shall kneel at your door at night; I shall hear your snore, your prayers, your dreams—and that shall be enough for me—I shall be your slave and your dog: I shall lie down at your feet, when you are awake, I shall keep watch with my dagger when night falls: and if one day, if one day you might love me—then! then!...'

"'Oh! leave me! leave me!...'

"'Eleonora! Eleonora! To lose nights and nights for one hope! To nurture it in my breast like a flower that withers from the cold— to nurture it, to revive it each day—only to see its petals shed before my face! To absorb myself in love and only have derision and scorn? Rather tell the painter to tear up his Madonna, tell the sculptor to shatter to pieces his statue of a woman.

"'Madwoman, poor madwoman that you are! do you believe that a man would let a thought take hold of his soul, live with that cancer, drink in the vitality of pain, only to tear it then away from his breast? Do you believe that he would consent to have his heart trampled on, to have the crown of his illusions stripped—him, poet and lover, of its flowers one by one? that on a disgraceful night, his insane motherly love could suffocate upon his breast the creature of his blood, the child of his life, the hope of his hopes?'

"'Oh! and won't you also take pity on me? Don't you know? this is dreadful! I'm a poor woman. On my knees I beg your forgiveness if I have offended you... I beg you, leave me alone! what do they matter to me, your dreams, your love?'

"That pain hurt me deeply: those tears burned me. But my will became as hard and iron-like as fate.

"'What do my dreams matter to you, what do my loves matter to you? Yes, you're right! What does the water of the desert, the gazelle of the sandy plain matter whether the Arab be thirsty or that the lion be hungry? But thirst and hunger are fatal. Love is like them.—Do you understand me now?'

"'Kill me, then! Won't you have a dagger? A stab, for the love of God! I swear, I will bless you...'

"'Dying! and you think of dying! Foolish woman!—to climb down from the warm bed of love to the cold stone of the dead! You don't know what you are saying. Do you know what that word is—dying? It is doubt that plagues existence: it is doubt, the premonition that cools the brow of the suicide, that passes through one's hairs like a winter wind, and pales our head like Hamlet's! Dying! it's the cessation of all dreams, of all palpitations of the chest, of all hopes! It's being chest to chest with our old loves and not feeling them!

You madwoman! it's a frightful betrothal, that of the worm: a very black sheet, that of the shroud! Don't you speak of that; why remember the gravedigger by the bed of life? put your hand upon your heart—it beats—and beats with strength, like the fetus in its mother's womb. There is still much life inside: much love for loving, much fire for living. Oh! if only you wanted to love me!'

"She hid her head in her hands and sobbed.

"'It's impossible: I cannot love you!'

"I said to her:

"'Eleonora, listen to me: I will leave you alone; however, I will watch over you from that door. Make up your mind: let it be a firm decision, yes, but well thought out. Mind that today you cannot return to the world: Duke Maffio would be the first to flee from you: he would feel the depravity of adultery on your face; he would believe he could feel the moisture of a stranger's kiss on your mouth. He would curse you! See: beyond lies but malediction and scorn: derision from other women, vindictive mockery from those who loved you and whom you did not love. When you enter, they will say, here she is! she has repented! her husband—poor him—has forgiven her... Mothers will hide their daughters from you: honest wives will be ashamed to touch you... And here, Eleonora, here you will have my heart and my love—a life for you only: a man who will only think of you and will always dream of you: a man whose world will be you, your laughs, your glances, your loves: who will forget *yesterday* and *tomorrow* to make you, like a God, his eternity. Think, Eleonora! if you wanted, we could depart today: a life of happiness awaits us. I am very rich, enough to adorn you like a queen.—We will tour Europe, we will go see France with its luxury, Spain, where the climate invites love, where afternoons are embalmed by the orange groves in bloom, where meadows are velvety and garnished with a thousand flowers; we will go to Italy, your homeland, and in your blue sky, in your limpid nights, in your gentlest twilights, live again under the southern sun!... If you want... otherwise it would be horrible... I don't know what would happen: but whoever entered this room would have their feet soaked in blood...'

"I left: two hours later I returned.

"'Have you thought about it, Eleonora?'

"She did not answer. She was lying with the face in her hands. At my voice she rose. There was a paper wet with her tears on the bed. I reached out to take it—she handed it to me.

"These were some verses of mine.—I looked at the table, my traveling bag, which I had brought from the carriage, was open: the papers were jumbled. These were the verses."

Claudius pulled a yellowed and crumpled piece of paper out of his pocket: he cast it on the table. Johann read:

Do not hate me, woman, if in the past
A dark stain turned my life awry,
When burning vice scorched my lips,
And I told it all with head held high.

The mask of Don Juan burned my face
With the cold pallor of the profligate:
That gaze withered me—and the cold lips
Dared to maledict my fate.

Aye! long nights in gambling fervor
Did I squander, febrile and haggard:
I gave away my prospects to a God of chance
And I profaned love with forgetfulness.

I withered with scorn the poet's crowns,
Love and glory with glum satire:
In the vapors of wine, the night insane
Pushed me towards the gambling fire!

I profaned the flower of my youth
In my past's slimy, muddy wave...
Fever in my skull, pallor on my face,
I only believed in the peaceful grave!

At the strumpet's breath I sickened
Wrapped in angel's wings of pure bliss:
Still my lips are purpled by the seal
    Of a trollop's kiss.

And the myrrh of songs no longer fades away
In a desecrated, stained, black goblet:
A sea of mud passed into the river of my soul,
My snowy flowers burst from my edges.
Dreams of glory only slyly come to me,
Like flowers opening fearfully on the ground
                                    of tombs
     —Gaunt and scentless...

My love... my breast does silence it:
I keep it deep inside—in the shadows of the
                                    shrine
Where the grassland did not thrive in the wild.
My love... was a vision of white robes
From the orgy to the door, cold and sobbing:
A holy lamp raised on a loathsome bed:
A Templar jar on the tavern's table:
A morning star reflecting, pale
     On the quagmire of crime.

Like the leper of the cities of old
I know you had fled in horror from my kiss:
I know, in the mad living of those crazy years,
I sullied my beliefs in dark insanity:
—Vestal, I prostituted your virgin forms
—I myself cast to the sea the leaves of the
                                    crown,
—I exchanged the rosy tunic of infancy
     For the mantle of orgies.

Oh! do not love me even! Well then! one day
Perhaps the Lord will say to rotting Lazarus:

Arise now from the lupanar of death,
Be revived afresh in purest living!
And I shall live anew: the moth
Flaps its wings, shakes them, shines
Shedding its black hue, the filthy slime
    Of the discolored larva.

Then, woman, I shall wake: from the mud
Where Satan spent the night with me,
Where yet warm his mold perfumed
Satiny nudity of snowy forms.
And blond harlot on her white breasts
Laid my livid brow in insomnia
The fever of voluptuousness led to thirst
    For the kisses sold.

And then I shall wake to the purest sun,
My brow fragrant with the auras of hope!
I shall lave me with faith in the golden waters
Of Magdalene in tears—and from the angel
Which God perhaps will grant me, bowed
                and silent
In the effluvia of love to sip a kiss,
    To die on those lips!

. . . . . . . . . . . . . . . . . . . . . . . . . . . . . . . . . . . . .
. . . . . . . . . . . . . . . . . . . . . . . . . . . . . . . . . . .

"She hushed: she wept and moaned.

"I drew near her: I knelt as if before God.

"'Eleonora, yes or no?'

"She turned her face away, wanted to speak—she interrupted herself at every syllable.

"'Wait, let me pray a little: perhaps the Madonna will pardon me.'

"I genuinely waited.—She knelt down.

"'Now...' said she, rising and holding her hand out to me.

"'So?'

"'I'll go with you.'

"And she fainted."

. . . . . . . . . . . . . . . . . . . . . . . . . . . . . . . . . . . .
. . . . . . . . . . . . . . . . . . . . . . . . . . . . . . . . . . .

Here ended the story of Claudius Hermann.

He lowered his head on the table: he spoke no more.

"Are you asleep, Claudius? by God! he's either drunk or dead!"

It was Archibald who interpellated him: he shook him with all his might.

Claudius lifted his head a little: he was emaciated: his eyes were sunken in a dark shadow.

"Leave me alone, you damned! leave me alone, by heaven or by hell! don't you see I'm sleepy—sleepy and very sleepy?"

"What about the story, the story?" cried Solfieri.

"What about Duchess Eleonora?" asked Archibald.

"That's true...the story. It seems to have slipped my mind. It seems to have been all a dream!"

"And the Duchess?"

"The Duchess?...I seem to have heard that name before... To hell with her, what does it matter to me?"

Then he wanted to proceed; but an invincible force detained him.

"The Duchess...it's true! But how could I forget all this which I cannot remember!... Take this weight off my head...verily they filled my skull with molten lead!...," and he beat on his pale head like a doctor beats on the chest of a dying man to find some echo of life.

"So?"

"Ha! Ha! Ha!" roared someone who had remained estranged from the conversation.

"Arnold! be quiet!"

"You be quiet, Solfieri! I will tell the end of the story."

It was Arnold, the fair-haired, who was waking up.

"Listen you all," he said.

"One day, Claudius came into his house. He found his bed drenched in blood: and in an obscure recess of the alcove a madman embracing a corpse. The corpse was Eleonora's: the madman you would hardly have recognized, so much had the agony disfigured him! It was a bristled, disheveled head, a greenish complexion, deep-set, dull eyes in which the flame of insanity flickered furtively, like the luminous emanation of marshes amidst the darkness…

"But he knew him… it was Duke Maffio…

"Claudius let out a laugh.—It was somber like insanity—cold as the sword of the angel of darkness. He fell onto the floor: livid and sweaty like agony: stiff as death…

"He was drunk like the late Patriarch Noah, the first lover of the vine, ignorant virgin up until then, and today prostitute of all mouths… drunk like Noah the first drunkard of whom history tells! He slept heavily and deeply like the Apostle St. Peter in the Garden of Olives… The fact is that both had supped the night before…"

Arnold spread his cape on the floor, and lay down upon it.

Some instants thereafter his baritone snores mingled with the mighty concert of the snores of the slumberers…

# VI

## Johann

Pour quoi? c'est que mon coeur au milieu des délices
D'un souvenir jaloux constamment oppressé
Froid au bonheur présent va chercher ses supplices
Dans l'avenir et le passé.
ALEX. DUMAS.[57]

---

[57] The second stanza of a poem ("A ***") used by
Alexandre Dumas as the introduction to his successful
Romantic play *Antony* (1831). Azevedo's epigraph does
not respect the original punctuation and capitalization.
The lines should read "Pourquoi? C'est que mon cœur, au
milieu des délices,/ D'un souvenir jaloux constamment
oppressé,/ Froid au bonheur présent, va chercher ses
supplices/ Dans l'avenir et le passé!"

"Now it's my turn! I too want to cast my coin into your urn: it's the green penny of the beggar: poor alms indeed!

"It was in Paris, in a billiard hall. I don't know whether the fire of the game had carried me away, or the *kirsch* and *curaçao*[58] had burnt my ideas too much… Playing against me was a lad: he was called Arthur.

"He had a fair and delicate figure like that of a maiden. A childlike rosy blush reddened his cheeks; but it was a pink of a diluted hue. Light fluff shaded his lip, and over the oval of his face a golden down loomed like the fuzz that covers the peach.

"My opponent needed one point to win. As for me, I don't know how many I needed: I only know that it was a lot: and therefore great composure was required, and much care in playing.

"I struck the ball.—At that moment the billiard table jolted… The blond lad, whether

[58] Kirsch (usually called kirschwasser in its country of origin, Germany) is a colorless brandy made from sour cherries. Curaçao is a liqueur made from bitter orange peel, originally from the Dutch Indies. It is also colorless, but the artificial color blue is added to make it look more exotic. Both were often mentioned in the early 19th century in connection with the bad habits of dissolute youth,

voluntarily or not, had propped himself against the table… The ball veered off course, changed direction: with that deviation I lost… Rage overwhelmed me. I advanced towards him. At my burning stare the youth shook his blond hair and smiled mockingly.

"That was too much! I walked towards him: a slap resounded. The agitated lad walked towards me with a dagger, but our friends restrained us.

"'This is a sailors' brawl. Now a duel, that's the fight for men of honor.'

"The lad ripped off a glove with his teeth, and threw it in my face. It was insult for insult, a tooth for a tooth: it had to be blood for blood.

Half an hour later I took his hand in cold blood and uttered into his ear:

"'Your weapons, sir?'

"'You shall know at the place.'

"'Your witnesses?'

"'The night and my weapons.'

"'The time?'

"'Now.'

"'The place?'

"'You shall come with me! wherever we stop, that will be the place…'

"'Very well, very well: I'm ready, let's go.'

"I offered him my arm and we left. Seeing us so calm in conversation, they believed some satisfaction was in order. One of those in attendance, however, understood us.

"He came to us and said:

"'Gentlemen, isn't there any way to reconcile you?'

"We both smiled.

"'This is childish,' he retorted.

"We didn't respond.

"'If you need a witness, I'm ready.'

"We both bowed.

"He understood us: he saw that our will was firm: he withdrew.

"We left.

. . . . . . . . . . . . . . . . . . . . . . . . . . . . . . . . . . . .
. . . . . . . . . . . . . . . . . . . . . . . . . . . . . . . . .

"A hotel was open. The lad led me inside.

"'I live here, come in,' he said.

"We entered.

"'Sir,' he said, 'there is no means of peace between us: a slap and a glove thrown in a man's face are stains that only blood washes away. It is, then, a duel to the death.'

"'To the death,' I repeated like an echo.

"'Well then: I have only two people in the world—my mother and... Wait a little.'

"The lad asked for paper, pen and ink. He wrote: the lines were few. Finishing the letter, he offered it to me to read.

"'Look, it's not treachery,' he said.

"'Arthur, I believe you: I don't want to read this paper.'

"I rejected the paper. Arthur closed the letter, sealed the wax with a ring he wore on his finger. Upon seeing the ring, a tear rolled down his face and fell upon the letter.

"'Sir, you are a man of honor. If I die, take this ring: in my pocket you will find a letter: you will entrust everything to... I will tell you later to whom...'

"'Are you ready?' I asked.

"'Not yet! before one of us dies, it is fair that the dying man toast the last twilight of life. Let us not be Abyssinians[59]: besides, the sun in its setting vermillion is still beautiful.'

The Rhine wine flowed in golden waters into the green crystal goblets. The lad stood up.

"'Sir, allow me to make a toast with you.'

"'To whom?'

"'It's a mystery—it's a woman, and the name of that whom one once pressed on the lips, whom one loves, is a secret. Won't you make it?'

"'As you wish,' said I.

"We touched our glasses. The lad went to the window. He poured a few drops of the Rhine wine into the night. We drank.

[59] Allusion to the old stereotype about Abyssinians (i.e., Ethiopians) being melancholy and fatalistic.

"'One of us has made his last toast,' said he. 'Good night to one of us: good bed and quiet sleep to the son of the earth!'

"He went to an escritoire, opened it: he took two pistols.

"'This is quicker,' he said. 'By the sword the agony is longer. One of them is loaded, the other is not. We shall pick them out at random. We'll fire at point-blank range.'

"'That's murder...'

"'Didn't we say that it was a duel to the death, that one of us should die?'

"'You have a point. But tell me: where shall we go?'

"'Come with me. On the first deserted corner on the outskirts. Any street corner is dark enough for two men of whom one has to kill the other.'

"At midnight we were outside the city. He put the two pistols on the ground.

"'Choose, but without touching them.'

"I chose.

"'Now let's go,' I said.

"'Wait: I have a cold presentiment: and a sighing voice moans in my chest. I want to pray... it's a longing for my mother.'

"He knelt down. At the sight of that lad on his knees—perhaps upon a tomb—I remembered that I too had a mother and a sister... and that I had forgotten them. As for lovers, my loves were like the thirst of street dogs, they were quenched by water or by mud... I had only loved lost women.

"'It's time,' he said.

"We walked face to face. The pistols touched our chests. The flintlocks burst: just one shot blasted: he dropped dead...

"'Take this,' murmured the dying man, and beckoned me to his pocket.

"I threw myself at him. He was drowning in blood. He writhed three times and grew cold... I took the ring from his finger. I stuck my hand in his pocket as he had instructed. I found two notes.

"The night was dark: I couldn't read them.

"I returned to the city. In the dim light of the first streetlamp I looked at the two notes. The first was the letter to his mother. The other was opened: I read it.

"'At one o'clock tonight, at 60, ... Street, on the first floor: you'll find the door open.

Yours, G.'

"There was no other signature.

"I didn't know what to think. I had an idea: it was an enormity.

"I went to the meeting. It was dark. I had on my finger the ring I had brought from the dead man... I felt a tiny satiny hand take me by the hand: I went upstairs. The door closed.

"It was a delightful night! The blond man's lover was a virgin! Poor Romeo! Poor Juliet! It seems those two children had spent the nights with infantile kisses and pure dreams!

(Johann filled his glass: he drank it, but he shuddered.)

"When I was to leave, I encountered a figure by the door.

"'Good evening, sir, I have long been waiting for you.'

"That voice appeared known to me. However, my head was spinning...

"I didn't answer: it was a singular case. I kept on going down: the figure followed me. When we reached the street door I saw the glint of a knife blade. I made a movement and its edge grazed my shoulder. The fight became terrible in the darkness. Two men who did not know each other, who had no idea of ever having seen each other in plain daylight, and who might not see each other again alive.

"The dagger slipped from his hands, lost in the dark: I subdued him. It was a hellish scene, a man in the darkness smothering the mouth of the other with his hand, suffocating his throat with his knee, and with his other hand groping in the shadow, in search of a piece of iron.

"At that moment I felt a horrible pain: cold and pain ran through my hand. The man had died suffocated, and in his agony he had

113

plunged his teeth into my flesh. It was at great cost that I freed my bleeding fleshless hand from the corpse's mouth. I stood up.

"As I left I tripped over a noisy object. I stooped to see what it was. It was a dark lantern.[60] I wanted to see who the man was. I lifted the lamp…

"Its last gleam bathed the head of the deceased… and went out…

"I couldn't believe it: it had been a fantastic dream, that whole night. I dragged the corpse by the shoulders… I took it across the pavement to the streetlamp, lifted the bloody hairs from the face… (a spasm of fear horribly contorted the narrator's face—he took his glass, went on to drink: his teeth chattered as if from the cold: the glass shattered against his lips).

"That man—you know! was blood of my blood, fruit of my mother's womb just like me—he was my brother: an idea passed before my eyes like an anathema. Anxiously I went upstairs. I entered. The maiden had fainted with fright when hearing the fight. She had the face as cold as marble. Her bare, virgin breasts were still and icy like those of a statue… I felt her snow-like, half-naked form amidst the rumpled garments, where infamy had sealed the stain of a lost flower.

[60] A dark lantern has a sliding shutter so that it can be made dark without extinguishing the candle inside.

"I opened the window; I took her there…

"Truly I am damned! Hey, Archibald, give me another glass, fill it with *cognac*, fill it to the brim! See: I'm cold, very cold: I tremble with chills and the sweat runs down my face! I want the fire of spirits! the burning of the brain to the vapor which dazes… I want to forget!"

"What's wrong, Johann? you're shivering like an old codger!"

"What's wrong? what's wrong! Don't you see? She was my sister!…"

# VII

## The Last Kiss of Love

Well Juliet! I shall lie with thee to night!
SHAKESPEARE,
ROMEO AND JULIET.[61]

---

[61] "Well, Juliet, I will lie with thee to-night" (*Romeo and Juliet* V, i, 34).

It was late at night: the banquet had ended. The revelers, stuffed, were sleeping in the darkness.

A light blazed suddenly through the cracks in the door. The door was opened. A woman in black entered. She was pale, and the light of a lantern, which she held aloft in her hand, fell palely on her face, and gave a singular gleam to her eyes. Perhaps she had once been a typical beauty, one of those images which make one blush with voluptuousness in the dreams of youth. But now, with her livid complexion, her bright eyes, her purple lips, her marble hands, and her garments, dark and dripping from the rain, you would rather have called her—the lost angel of madness.

The woman bent down: with the lantern in her hand she searched among those sleeping faces for a familiar face.

When the light fell on Arnold, she knelt. She wanted to give him a kiss, she stretched her lips… But an idea stopped her. She stood up. When she reached Johann, who was sleeping, a smile whitened her lips: her gaze became somber.

She knelt beside him: she deposed the lamp on the floor. The dim flame of the lantern, falling on her clothes, spread a shadow over Johann. The woman's brow drooped, and her hand brushed against his throat.—A sob, raucous and choked, escaped from there. The stranger stood up. She trembled, and as she held the lantern, a piece of iron resounded in her hand... it was a dagger... she threw it on the floor. He saw her hands were red—she wiped them on Johann's long hair...

She turned back to Arnold; she shook him.

"Wake up and get up!"

"What do you want from me?"

"Look at me: don't you know me?"

"You! but isn't it a dream? It's you! oh! let me hold you still! Five years without seeing you! Five years! And how you have changed!"

"Yes: I am no longer as beautiful as I was five years ago! It is true, my blond lover! The flower of beauty is like all other flowers. Nourish them with the dew of virginity, with the wind of purity, and they will be beautiful.—Roll them in the mud—and like fallen fruit, they plunge into the sea, wrapped in something impure and brackish! Once this was Giorgia the virgin: but now it is Giorgia, the prostitute!"

"My God! my God!"

And the lad buried his brow in his hands.

"Do not curse me, no!"

"Oh! let me remember; these five years which have passed were a dream. That man from the billiard hall, the duel at point-blank range, my waking in a hospital, that dissolute life into which despair had thrown me, is this a dream! Oh! let us remember the past! When winter darkens the sky, let us shut our eyes; poor dying swallows, let us remember spring!..."

"Your words pain me... It is a farewell, it is a kiss of farewell and separation which I come to ask from you: on earth our bed would be impure, the world has tainted our bodies. The love of the libertine and the prostitute! Satan would laugh at us. It is in Heaven, when the tomb washes us in its bath, that our morning of love will rise..."

"Oh! to see you only to leave you once again! And haven't you thought, Giorgia, that it would have been better for me to die devoured by dogs in the empty street, whence they carried me full of blood? That it would have been better for you to murder me in my drunken sleep, than to point out to me the errant star of fortune while putting out the one in the sky? Haven't you thought that, after five years, five years of fever and insomnia, of waiting and despairing, of living for you, of yearning and agony, it would be hell to see you only to leave you?"

"Compassion, Arnold! It is necessary that this farewell be as long as life itself. You see, my fate is dark: in my memories there

121

is a vile stain... today! it is the venal bed... tomorrow!... I only hope for the bed of the tomb! Arnold! Arnold!"

"Do not call me Arnold! call me Arthur, like before. Arthur! don't you hear? Call me that! It has been so long since I last heard myself called by that name!... I was a madman: I wanted to drown my thoughts, and I wandered through cities and mountains, leaving everywhere my tears—in solitary caves, in silent fields, and on tables soaked with wine! Come, Giorgia! sit here, sit on my knees, nestled close to my heart... your head on my shoulder! Come! a kiss! I want to feel once more the perfume I once breathed on your lips. Let me breathe it in and die!... Five years! oh! such a long time waiting for you, longing for an hour in your arms!... Then... listen... I have so much to say to you! so many tears to shed in your lap! Come! and I shall tell you my whole story! My illusions of lover, and the cursed nights of debauchery, and the tedium which inspired in me those cold lips of the prostitutes who kissed me! Come! I shall tell you all this: I shall tell you how I have profaned my soul, and my past: and we shall weep together—and our tears will wash us clean as the rain washes the mud off the leaves!"

"Thank you, Arthur! thank you!"

The woman choked on her tears, and the young man murmured words of love between kisses.

"Listen, Arthur! I only came to say goodbye! from the edge of my grave: and then, content, I would close its door myself... Arthur, I am going to die!"

They both wept.

"Now look," she continued. "Come with me: do you see that man?"

Arnold took the lantern.

"Johann! dead! for the blood of God! who killed him?"

"Giorgia! He was a wicked man. It was he who left for dead a young man whom he had slapped in a gambling house. Giorgia the prostitute took revenge on him, Giorgia the virgin. It was this man who had dishonored her! dishonored her, she who was his sister!"

"The horror! the horror!"

And the young man turned his face away and covered it with his hands.

The woman knelt down at his feet.

"And now farewell! farewell, for I am dying! Don't you see that I am livid, that my eyes grow dim, and I tremble... and faint?"

"No! I will not leave. If I live tomorrow, there will be horrible memories in my past..."

"And aren't you afraid? Look! it is death that comes! it is life that is fading on my brow. Don't you see this shiver between my eyebrows?..."

"And what does it matter to me, the dream of death? My future tomorrow would be terrible: and on the rotting head of the corpse no memories resound; death glues its lips together; the grave is silent. I will die!"

The woman faltered... faltered. The young man took her in his arms, pressed his lips to hers... She gave a scream, and fell from his hands. It was horrible to see. The young man took the dagger, closed his eyes, thrust it into his chest, and fell upon her. Two groans were concealed by the thud of a falling body...

The lamp went out.

## [THE END.]

---

www.ingramcontent.com/pod-product-compliance
Lightning Source LLC
Chambersburg PA
CBHW041605240626
47164CB00008B/180